blood

blood

BOOK ONE OF THE MERCIAN TRILOGY

K. J. WIGNALL

HIGH SCHOOL LIBRARY
GLASTONBURY, CT

EGMONT

USA

New York

EGMONT

We bring stories to life

First published in the United Kingdom by Egmont UK Ltd, 2011
First published in the United States of America by Egmont USA, 2011
443 Park Avenue South, Suite 806
New York, NY 10016

Copyright © K. J. Wignall, 2011
All rights reserved

10 9 8 7 6 5 4 3 2 1

www.egmontusa.com

Library of Congress Cataloging-in-Publication Data

Wignall, Kevin.
Blood / K.J. Wignall.
p. cm.—(Mercian trilogy ; bk. 1)
    Summary: A centuries-old vampire wakes up in the modern day to find he is
being hunted by an unknown enemy, and begins to uncover the secrets of his
origin and the path of his destiny.
ISBN 978-1-60684-220-1 (hardcover)
ISBN 978-1-60684-258-4 (electronic book)
[1. Vampires—Fiction. 2. Good and evil—Fiction.] I. Title.
PZ7.W63939Bl 2011
[Fic]—dc22
                          2011005899

Printed in the United States of America

CPSIA tracking label information:
Printed in August 2011 at Berryville Graphics, Berryville, Virginia
Book design by Arlene Schleifer Goldberg

All rights reserved. No part of this publication may be reproduced, stored in a retrieval
system, or transmitted, in any form or by any means, electronic, mechanical, photo-
copying, or otherwise, without the prior permission of the publisher and copyright
owner.

blood

1

We burned the witches in 1256. It was the last time I really enjoyed a fire—not because of the witches, you understand, even though I was for burning them at the time—just for the pleasure of flames dancing in the night sky and filling the land with their orange glow.

I've never looked at fire in the same way since that night, nor witches for that matter, or anybody else who's *apart*. Perhaps apart is the wrong word, for I was apart even then, in that I was above the people and below God and the King, born into greatness.

Had I not fallen sick, I would have become . . . But there is no use in talking about what I would have become because I did fall sick and my younger half-brother wrongfully inherited the Earldom, and now he and all his noble line across hundreds of years are long since reduced to dust, the line itself extinct.

Apart is definitely the wrong word—what I understand is the outcast, for that is surely what happened to me when the sickness struck. I was cast out. I was removed from the comfort of my family and friends, from my home, sentenced to a lifetime of darkness, existing between worlds.

If we had not returned from Marland Abbey where we had been in the days previously, my fate might have been avoided. But of course we did return, to see justice done, for the Earl to be seen to deliver his people from their suffering. We returned because that night was ours, our triumph over witchcraft and evil.

I do not remember being bitten. I wish I did, for then I would know the face of the creature who did this to me, and I would have a purpose, to track him down and repay him for the poisoned gift he gave me. But as much as I have tried, the memory of the attack has never returned and I have remained taunted by his absence.

Nor do I remember anything of what happened in the days following my infection, but the years have at least allowed me to piece together some fragment of those events, of the fear and panic that surely reigned in our household at that time.

They thought I was dead, that much is certain, cursed by some devilry. Perhaps they even blamed the witches who were still being reduced to tallow even as my body was found. Whatever fear possessed them, I was probably interred in haste in the crypt, but did not rest, and in the days or weeks following, I was placed in a casket and buried beneath the city walls.

And I was at peace there. The casket rotted around me, but my body remained unchanged. If my father at the end of his life, or my brother at the end of his, had troubled themselves to dig in that withered spot, they would have found my skin unblemished, my flesh untouched by time or worms.

In the year of 1256, the year of my sickness, I was sixteen years old, not as young in that time as it is now. I was tall, too, enough that I was already being called Will Longshanks.

I'm tall even now for my age. I say "my age" because, for all the passing of nearly eight hundred years, I am still sixteen in my person, just as I will be sixteen when you who read this are old, then dead, then forgotten.

2

The more that's known about the world, the more people seem determined to search for what is lost or hidden. There are archaeologists, treasure hunters, and ghost hunters—the legions of the curious—searching for secrets and the places that hold them. They ignore the possibility that some secrets are best kept, some places better left untouched—this bare room, for example, with its one ancient artifact.

It was an open stone casket, buried up to the lip in compacted soil and filled with looser earth. An archaeologist, stumbling upon it, would first have excavated around its sides to reveal the intricate carvings with which it had been adorned. From this they'd have dated it and come to the conclusion that it had belonged to someone of high birth.

The same archaeologist, excited now and ignoring obvious questions—such as why this casket was buried so close to the surface in a hidden chamber deep beneath the city walls—would carefully begin to remove the looser earth, hoping to find the body of the nobleman who'd been interred there.

Regrettably, such an archaeologist wouldn't live to tell the tale because the "nobleman" inside was not dead, but merely at rest.

In the darkness now, the soil inside the casket began to stir and, a moment later, a figure emerged as gracefully as someone might surface from the water in a bath, his face appearing first, then his upper body and arms. He placed his hands on the sides of the casket, as he had done many times over the previous eight centuries, and pushed himself clear of the earth, stepping out on to the firm surface of the chamber floor.

He stood for a second and felt the inside of his right forearm, instinctively searching for wounds that he knew had long disappeared. As he did this, he breathed in deeply through his nose, his acute sense of smell dissecting the air for any sign of life. His senses confirmed what he also already knew, that he was alone there, and he relaxed and walked along the short passageway to the neighboring chamber.

He lit candles, preparing his eyes for the violent lights he knew he'd encounter in the world above. But even the dusty yellow flames seemed to burn his retinas, and he closed his eyelids against the stinging glare, opening them little by little until his vision adjusted.

So there he stood, naked and white-skinned, a boy of sixteen, but looking a little older, already tall and muscled. His hair, still disheveled and dirty from the soil, was dark and wild and long enough to reach his shoulders. His fingernails and toenails were long, too, as if they'd kept growing, albeit slowly, during his hibernation.

His name was Will, short for William, though he couldn't easily remember the last time anyone had called him by that or any other name. Nor had he ever been addressed by his true title, for by rights, since his father's death in the winter of 1263, the boy standing in the dulled candlelight had been, and always would be, William, Earl of Mercia.

As soon as his eyes had adjusted, he picked up one of the candlesticks and carried it through into a third chamber, not because he needed it to see the way, but because he didn't want to be reacquainted with the smarting pain of light every time he came back into the room. To be in the light was always a discomfort, but he was used to it now and so it was better to stay that way.

The third chamber was the least like a room. For the most part, it was a natural cave into which an opening had been made. On the far side, an underground spring trickled into a small pool, the water flowing away from there through a small crevice into some deeper channel.

Will settled the candlestick and stepped down into the pool. The water was winter cold, but its temperature hardly registered with him—it was water, nothing more, a liquid for washing away the dust that clung to his skin and hair. It took him only a few minutes and then he stepped out.

He picked up the candlestick and walked a fading trail of wet footprints back into the main chamber. He opened the chests on the far side of the room and stared at them, almost as if reminding himself of the contents. Yet, despite the years he'd lain dormant, it was all as familiar to him as after a day's rest.

If he'd been pale before bathing, his skin was now bordering on translucent. Rather than dry himself, he took scissors and cut the nails on his fingers and toes. He trimmed a small amount from his hair, too, leaving it long.

Finally, he took a cloth and dried the remaining water from his skin. Then, almost as an afterthought, he reached into one of the chests and drew out a looking glass. He held it up and studied his own reflection.

Over the last two centuries, since stories about people like him had become popular, he'd read on many occasions that he would produce no reflection in a mirror. Perhaps others would see nothing of his reflection, but he'd never failed to see himself and, like so many of the myths that surrounded his kind, it amused him that people were so far from knowing the truth of his condition.

His features were fine, befitting a nobleman, his eyes were green, his skin soft and smooth. Though he was adult for his age in other regards, he'd produced not even the beginnings of a beard at the time of his sickness. It had troubled him for the first hundred years or more, showing him up for the youth he was, but he'd long since come to appreciate the convenience of not having to deal with shaving.

But Will wasn't staring into the glass to admire his own face. He opened his mouth, revealing the long canines that had once again grown into fangs, the lower set smaller, the uppers long enough to puncture flesh.

He looked at them and felt a mild frustration that they had returned during the years he'd been at rest. As was often the case with corpses he'd seen unearthed, it was his hair and nails and teeth that continued to grow while the rest of him was frozen in time.

He took a file and carefully set to work on the four pronounced fangs, grinding them back down to something that resembled those of normal people. The file made a metallic grating sound against the enamel of his teeth, and the action vibrated through him and filled his mouth with powdery debris, but he felt no pain.

When he'd finished, he dropped the file back into the chest, went to the pool, and washed the bone dust from his mouth. He dressed then, black boots and trousers, a black shirt, a long black coat—he had no way of knowing if it would look appropriate, but it had been plain enough for him to blend in from 1813 onwards and he had to assume it would still suffice. He took a handful of items from another chest and placed them in the pockets of his coat, and at last he was ready.

It had taken him the best part of an hour, not bad considering the sleep from which he'd recently woken, but he was becoming impatient. He could sense that night had fallen in the city far above, and he knew that before he did anything else, he needed to feed. It was unfortunate that it always had to start like this, that someone had to die for the benefit of his well-being, but that was the nature of his sickness. He needed blood.

3

Will picked up the large block of stone that sealed the entrance to his chamber and moved it to one side. He walked along the passageway, passing the partially collapsed chamber into which he'd first fallen centuries earlier. At first, the passage followed the line of the city wall, but then turned abruptly, and he knew that he was now under the church and that the steps were only a short way ahead of him.

He reached them and ascended, absentmindedly counting the forty steps, and as he neared the top, he reached up with his hands to touch the stone slab above his head. He crouched down under it and waited for a moment, his palms pressed against it.

Only when he sensed the absence of life in the room above did he push the heavy stone up and across the floor of the crypt. From his crouching position he leapt up, emerging between the tombs of his father and brother.

He eased the stone back into place and walked to the outer gate, which was locked. The last time he'd emerged from hibernation had been in 1980, a period of activity which had lasted only nine years. It had been the first time in more than seven hundred years that he'd found the crypt gate and the church door locked, and whatever year it was now, the times were clearly still lawless.

Will put his hand over the lock and closed his eyes, channeling his energy into the metal. He felt the mechanism slowly freeing itself before the gate opened in his hand. He closed it again behind him and climbed the steps into the church, but halted, sensing immediately that there were people ahead, even though he couldn't see them.

A moment later, he heard some laughter, the wooden echo of a door closing, and the ascent of steps. He stood still and waited, listening. He could hear papers being sorted, and then a few soft notes emerged from the organ.

As restless as he was, as mentally fatigued, it soothed Will to hear the haunting lull of music, but his pleasure didn't last long. A woman appeared at the far end of the nave and stared in his direction. She walked towards him, an air of angry authority about her, and when she was still some way distant she said, "What do you think you're doing in here?"

He'd sensed this the last time, too, the assumption by adults that anyone of his apparent age would be about some criminal purpose. It was an odd view to take, he thought, and this woman's tone was so unpleasant that he regretted she wouldn't make a suitable feed.

If a woman like this was found murdered, the authorities would search for the killer and, sooner or later, one of those searches would find him. He never preyed on people who'd be missed, who mattered. It was easier to feed off the plentiful supply of people who mattered to no one.

Will watched as she approached. He imagined she was fifty—short gray hair, wide-hipped, and full of figure in a tweed skirt and knitted cream sweater. Clearly she had nothing better to do than feel important in God's house and carry out minor acts of tyranny.

She was almost upon him, determined to give him a telling-off for being there, but she looked into his eyes and he stared back and she ground abruptly to a halt. She didn't seem to know what to say—here was a boy, she had probably thought, a boy who was up to no good, but now that she was locked into the hidden world of his eyes she was no longer sure of anything.

She offered a weak smile and said apologetically, "The cathedral's closed, I'm afraid. From six o'clock on winter

Tuesdays. I suppose you didn't hear the announcement—easily done." He still didn't speak. "Er, yes, if you follow me, I'll be happy to show you out."

Will took a step towards her. She looked full of fear, but couldn't move herself or speak. He took hold of her hand, his finger touching the underside of her wrist, the pulse of her blood sending a desperate hunger through him.

She moved her mouth, but no words came out, and with his free hand he reached up and put a finger on her lips. In the background, the organist started to play a louder, more uplifting piece, the notes reverberating through the air, and though his words would be drowned out, Will knew she would understand because, at this moment, she could hear and see only him. Everything else, the world she knew, had entirely fallen away.

"I will be visiting a great deal in the near future. I will become such a familiar sight that you won't notice me at all. I will be invisible to you."

The woman's eyes flickered—it was as much of a response as she could manage. Will let go of her hand and left her standing there, knowing that by the time she came back to herself, she would remember him only like a broken dream.

He left by the side door, but was instantly blinded by floodlights and the piercing headlights of cars. For a minute or so, he could do nothing but stand still, trying not to scream out with the pain that burned through his eyes.

He'd instinctively closed his eyelids against the glare, but there was no stopping all this light. He didn't wait for his eyes to adjust this time, but as soon as he was able to open them even a sliver, he stumbled forwards and headed as quickly as possible for the darker backstreets.

It was a winter Tuesday and it was after six, the woman in the church had told him that much, but the city was still thronged with tourists, and even the backstreets were full of visual hazards. He hadn't wanted to do this, but he reached into his overcoat pocket and took out a pair of dark glasses.

The city was brighter than it had been last time and his eyes would take longer to adjust, if they adjusted at all. But with the glasses on, the pain eased enough for him to open his eyes fully again and see clearly what lay around him.

The clothes of the people were not much different from the last time and, while he saw no one dressed exactly as he was, nobody stared at him, except for the occasional glance towards his dark glasses.

He was troubled though, because he could smell blood all around him, and he'd smell it that strongly until he satisfied his need. Until he fed, he wouldn't be able to move easily among people.

Will made for the South Gate, and from there into the derelict area that led down to the river. The time before last, 1920 to 1938, this Victorian warehouse district had been thriving, even at night, but the last time it had fallen into decay and become home to vagrants and drug users—people who wouldn't be missed.

It hadn't changed. Will stopped outside the second gutted warehouse and breathed deeply, the scent of his victim immediately flaring in his nostrils. He put his glasses back in his pocket and pushed through the gap in the boarded-up doors.

It was a long, low building under a gently peaked roof, only one story. The whole space was open and dark, but there was a small partially enclosed office at the far end, and through the openings where its windows had been, he could see the dim flickering of candlelight.

He walked quickly and stood in the office doorway. The little room was now a makeshift home, with charcoal pictures hanging on the walls, books stacked up on crates and shelves, an old mattress, and various grubby clothes and blankets and sleeping bags.

There was a small stove in the corner, the one remaining part of the original office's comfort, a black pipe rising from it and up through the roof. The stove was lit and two wiry black dogs lay dozing in front of it.

On the other side of the room, sitting cross-legged on the mattress, was a man with matted brown hair and a beard. He was barefoot, wearing khaki trousers and a thick top, which had once been pale blue, but now appeared to have grime in every one of its fibers. There were beads and bangles around both of his wrists, and a leather bracelet around one of his ankles.

The man was writing in a notebook by the light of three large candles, but he stopped now and looked up. He was surprised but not alarmed to see Will standing there.

Will was surprised, too, because the man's face was young beneath his beard and scraggly hair. He was young and healthy and, judging by the many books, educated, too, so Will found it hard to understand how his circumstances could have been so reduced.

The man spoke and his voice was soft and distracted, as if he had to keep calling himself back from some distant place. "Hey, man, I didn't see you there." He looked towards the stove and said, "Weird that the dogs didn't hear you coming—they're normally bang on."

Will stepped inside without answering, avoiding a waist-high stack of magazines just inside the door. He picked one up and looked at it before saying, "What is this?"

"It's the *Big Issue*, man. I'm a seller." Will didn't comprehend, even though he could see the name of the publication. "You must've heard of it. You must have seen people selling it in the street." The man seemed intrigued now and put his notebook to one side, staring at Will. "You don't seem like the usual kind of runaway—what's your story?"

Will was still looking at the magazine and said, "Is this the date?"

"Yeah, it's this week's."

It should have been obvious to him because he'd already come to the conclusion that he'd slept for at least ten years, but even so, Will was shocked at the realization that this was the twenty-first century.

He'd found himself in new centuries many times before, but the thought of being adrift in a new millennium was troubling somehow. He imagined the next thousand years stretching out ahead of him, saw himself a prisoner to this half-life across ten more centuries, then another, and another. The only thing he couldn't imagine was why, to what purpose?

"Look, man, whatever your problem is, it's cool, you know." Will dropped the magazine back on the pile and stared at him. "I'm Jex, and trust me, I've seen and heard everything, man, and it's all cool."

Will had never heard such a name before—Jex. Jex, who thought he'd seen and heard everything.

He continued to stare and said, as a matter-of-fact, "I could tell you some things you haven't heard before."

Jex started to laugh, perhaps thinking it funny that this boy thought he knew more of the world than him, but then he made eye contact and stopped with the sound still unformed in his throat. Within a moment, he'd become mesmerized by the intensity of Will's gaze.

Will took another step forwards and knelt down in front of him. He took the young man's hand and pushed up the grubby blue sleeve of his top. Jex looked down at his own forearm and then back at Will, already totally within his power, no less than a fly paralyzed by a spider's venom.

Will held the wrist, just above the assorted bangles and bracelets, then took a small knife from the pocket of his overcoat and cut a short, neat line up the arm. As the blood started to flow, his instinct was to lap it up urgently, so great was his need, but just as he was about to lock his mouth around the wound, Jex spoke from deep within his trance.

"He's calling."

Despite his hunger for blood, Will sat back on his haunches and stared at Jex in shock. This didn't happen: his victims did not speak once they were entranced. And Jex was still hypnotized, but he had definitely spoken, a fact that unnerved Will more than perhaps it should have done.

"Who?"

Jex's eyes were fixed on the point in space where Will had stood, and he showed no signs of having heard him, but even so, he responded mechanically, saying, "Lorcan Labraid. He calls."

"Who is Lorcan Labraid?"

Jex's head shook with a fearful tremor, as if he didn't want to hear what he could hear, as if he didn't want to speak, but could not stop himself. "Lorcan Labraid? He is the evil of the world. And he calls you." He slumped back a little, apparently exhausted, mumbling, "You need the girl, the girl needs you, you need the . . ."

Will stared at him for a second or two more, intrigued even as he tried to dismiss the words as those of a dying man, but he could wait no longer, distracted by the rich scent of the blood. He lowered his head to the wound and took the liquid as it pumped gently from the torn flesh.

He felt better almost instantly with the metallic warmth filling his mouth. He'd long understood that this wasn't food—he didn't need blood the way he'd once needed meat or bread. It was something else that he took from it, as if he was draining the life force itself from his victims.

He didn't need blood all the time. He needed it most when he first emerged from hibernation. After that, he could go weeks or even months without the need for more, and the need wasn't a bodily hunger, but a spiritual one.

He was never physically weak for want of blood, but sometimes before he fed, it felt as if every last fragment of his soul was floating away and dispersing into the void. Only blood brought it back.

Within forty minutes it was done. Jex lay on the mattress now, both arms exposed, two cuts on each, and the blood continued to seep weakly out of the wounds. Will hadn't drained him and had stopped drinking as soon as the life had left him.

He stood and looked around the room. For a moment, he thought back to the strangeness of Jex talking through his trance and of the things he'd said—Lorcan Labraid, the evil of the world, something about a girl— but the room alone was enough to convince him that Jex had taken drugs aplenty in his time, that his mind had been unhinged even though his body had remained healthy.

The dogs were still sleeping, unaware that he was there or what fate had befallen their master. The stove was burning low and orange, and if Jex had been still alive, he might have put more wood on it.

He looked at the charcoal pictures then. They were well drawn, some of the dogs, some of faces, including a girl who looked cross and unhappy, many of the city itself, some of the church. Again, it surprised and even saddened him that a young man of talents had come to live like this.

Will felt a little saddened, too, for having ended that life, but it was the nature of his sickness. Besides, millions of people had died during his long existence, and many of them had lost their lives far more pointlessly than the man in front of him now.

Will spotted the notebook that Jex had been writing in and picked it up, thumbing idly through the pages. He probably would have thrown it aside again, but as he looked through it, his forearm started to itch, on the exact spot where he'd once been bitten himself.

It was a sensation he'd never experienced before, the second new experience in one night, and once again, he started to think seriously about the things Jex had said. Could it be that Lorcan Labraid was the name of the creature who'd bitten him, and that through the flaring up of this ancient wound, he was indeed calling to Will?

He even wondered if the itching was somehow linked to the simple act of picking up the notebook. It was hard to believe this book could have any connection with the creature who'd infected him so long ago, but even the slightest promise of it was enough to pique Will's interest.

Most of the pages were filled with dense script, but there were drawings, too. Much of the writing was in a tight scrawl that was hard for him to read, and nonsensical where he could, but here and there notes were written in large capital letters.

As he flicked through the pages, his eyes fixed on one of these bold statements. Two words in particular had leapt out at him as they'd flashed past, words he couldn't believe he'd seen. Surely his eyes had deceived him. He turned back, a page at a time, his heart lurching.

Then he reached it and read it again, one simple but shocking sentence, written bold, the words underlined. And there were the two words in particular that had caught his attention, words that could have no reason for being in this man's notebook—*William . . . Mercia.*

He tried to take in the meaning of them appearing there and of the sentence that carried them, but felt a sudden sharp discomfort on his forearm, deep in the tissue—not itching now, but the sensation of two teeth sinking into his flesh. He had to be imagining it, or remembering it, dredging up a memory that he'd never knowingly possessed. It got worse—a needle-like pain tore through his flesh, a pain so alarming, so disturbing that Will dropped the book and stumbled, kicking one of the crates.

The dogs stirred and jumped up, starting to growl, but uncertain what to do. A candle toppled and rolled across the crate before dropping to the floor, the flame catching under the edge of the blanket that covered the mattress.

Will recoiled instantly from the fire, as small as it was. One of the dogs barked at him, then the other, maybe sensing his moment of weakness. He turned and glared at them and they quietened, looking hesitant, then sloped one after the other out the door.

The blanket had started to burn properly by the time he turned back to it, smoke billowing upwards, the flames dancing against everything they touched, trying to take hold. Then he spotted the notebook lying on the mattress next to Jex, the edges of its pages already beginning to singe and crackle.

Will had never been burned, but just as some sicknesses could make their victims fear water, so he feared the flames, no less than if he were a wild animal. He'd learned to live with the careful, controlled fire of the candle, but this kind of flame, volatile and fast and greedy, made him almost as uneasy as the first glint of light at the edge of every morning.

But he knew what he'd seen in that book and the sensations it had stirred in him, and he couldn't let it burn. He kicked it clear of the flames and stamped on it, making certain that it was no longer alight before daring to pick it up.

He slipped the book into the pocket of his coat and ran from the fire, out into the freshening night where he halted again. A wind had picked up, whipping through the old warehouses, carrying broken sounds from here and there in the city, tugging violently at his hair and coat.

The night seemed volatile and in fear of itself, as if something had just been unleashed into the darkness, perhaps by his killing of Jex, or by his discovery of the book, or both. Whatever had happened in there, Will could sense that something had shifted in his nocturnal world—things were not the same as they'd been an hour before.

He put his hand into his pocket, reassuring himself that the notebook was still there, but almost instantly the wind dropped and the crisp calmness of the night settled back on to the city. He could hear only the faint crackling of the flames now, and the distant traffic that would soon bring a fire engine.

Before finding the book, he'd wanted to walk and breathe air he hadn't breathed for more than a decade, to clear his thoughts. Now he wanted only to go back to his chamber so that he could read and decipher everything Jex had written, to understand something of what was happening and the things of which he'd spoken.

But Will hadn't even started to walk again when he heard a noise from the direction of the river. He stared into the darkness and saw the two dogs, running at full speed. At first he thought they were running back to their master, but they sprinted past, determined, not even noticing Will. The look and the smell of them were unmistakable—they were running away from something in fear for their lives.

He looked back in the direction from which they'd come, and without giving it any further thought, he set off towards the river. If there was something down there that had scared the dogs, he wanted to see it, and as he walked, his heart was full of the nervous blood of hope.

He'd lived in ignorance for nearly eight hundred years, understanding little of his sickness, gathering fragments from the superstitions of others. Nor, in all that time, had he ever met another of his own kind, but finally in this notebook, in the words of a dead man, there was perhaps a sign.

At last, in this new millennium, he'd found a message in the most unlikely of places. And it promised something that he'd never dared hope, that there had been a reason for all of this, his sickness, the centuries of loneliness, that he had a destiny.

There was something else, too, in the aching of his arm, in the way the darkness had become possessed, in the terror of the dogs, a tantalizing suggestion that the book would lead him to the one who'd made him what he was. Will rested his hand on the book now, and was almost afraid to hope that their meeting might be imminent—for after all, the dogs had run from something, or someone.

4

All the way to the river, the dull ache remained in his arm, reminding Will that he had been cursed with this existence, born of wickedness, reminding him, too, that whatever had come back into his life in this last hour was also wicked. And with Jex's words still in his mind, it was evil he expected to find at the river.

What he actually found there was a scene of confusion, a scene of dereliction lost. The first riverside warehouse he saw was surrounded by scaffolding and appeared to be undergoing some building work. The next one, a large four-story block that stretched all the way to the road and the bridge, had been converted into living accommodation, as had the one on the opposite bank.

Will stared at the buildings, unable to take in what was happening here. He looked up at the lit windows, at the people moving about their domestic business. It was a strange choice of place to live, he thought. If the creature who'd bitten him was anywhere here, it would not be among the living.

Instinctively, he turned and walked the other way along the river, away from the light and signs of life, further into the small island of desolation which it seemed he was already on the verge of losing.

He hadn't walked far when he sensed someone up ahead and his hope faded of finding the creature tonight, for this was a healthy living person. If she, for he sensed it was a she, was unharmed and unafraid then it was unlikely the creature was close by. With even more disappointment, he wondered if the dogs had been spooked by nothing so much as their own shadows. Even so, he walked on.

He couldn't see her, not even when he knew he was close, and he was only a few steps away when he finally spotted her, sitting on the floor inside the deep doorway of what had once been a coffee merchant's.

She looked no older than him, her skin was almost as pale, her raven hair even darker than his, and she, too, was dressed all in black, albeit with silver rings on nearly every finger.

The girl was beautiful and sad, but more importantly,

Will recognized her and became hopeful again that he'd been drawn here for a reason. Because this was the girl whose picture had been on the wall of Jex's hovel. "The girl needs you, you need the girl," that was what he'd said, or something like it. Had he meant this girl?

"What are you staring at?"

Her tone was hostile and Will had been distracted, not even realizing that he was staring. "I'm sorry, I didn't mean to."

She ignored the apology, leaving no opening for conversation. Will scratched absentmindedly at his arm, not because it was itching now, but because he could still remember the discomfort so clearly.

"Are you a junkie?"

Her tone was accusatory and he dropped his hand and said earnestly, "No. Something bit me, that's all."

"Charming," she said sarcastically. He wasn't sure how to respond, but a moment later she added, "So? Go away. Leave me alone."

He was a little taken aback by her unfriendliness and by the determined way she spoke, as if it didn't occur to her that he might disobey. But he quickly realized that it was a front, a defensive mechanism to fend people off.

"This is a public space," he said, and even now, even after all this time, a voice inside his head corrected him— it was *his* space, belonging to him by right, just as all the land hereabout belonged to him.

She changed her tactics, but it was clear she didn't want to talk to him. "Maybe it is, but it's not a good place for you to be. You should go home to your parents."

Her tone was mocking and full of contempt, but he ignored it and said, "What do you mean, it's not a good place? Have you seen anything strange down here?"

"Yeah, loads of things, so you know what? Go home, get a life."

She was definitely mocking him, but as ever, it was taking him a little while to get used to the words and rhythm of the language. As he tried to understand what she'd said, he noticed her shiver slightly.

"You're cold."

"It's a cold night—it has been known in November." Will nodded. He was conscious of the crispness in the air, but didn't feel it in his bones as he would once have done. She tried another tactic, saying, "Look, I don't mean to be rude, but please just leave me alone."

"Of course. It wasn't my intention to intrude." He took a step backwards, but before turning he said, "And I'm an orphan."

"Oh." She seemed to think about it a second before saying, "How long?"

"A long time."

The girl nodded, still not giving any ground, but said, "That's too bad."

Will turned and walked away. This wasn't the right time, but she had at least spoken to him and he would have

29

all the time he needed. It was unfortunate that she'd been so unfriendly because he'd liked the way she looked—if it hadn't been for her scent, he might even have taken her for one of his own.

More important was that her picture had been on Jex's wall, and that Jex had talked about a girl immediately after he'd spoken of Lorcan Labraid. So possibly it was no coincidence that Will had found her. If greater powers were at work, maybe there would be no more coincidences—he had been lured to the river, and he had found a girl there.

A fire engine had reached the warehouse and was in the process of putting out the fire, which was intense but contained at the far end. He put his dark glasses on and, as he passed, one of the firemen turned and laughed, saying, "Too sunny for ya?"

Will paid no attention and walked on. It was one of his curses that men like that would talk down to him because he was a boy. If they knew only a fraction of the truth, about his age or his power, they would bow down before him no less than their long-distant grandfathers had done.

He returned the way he'd come and entered the church through the side door. He'd been away nearly two hours, but there were still people in there, even if the music had now stopped and the cavernous silence had once more returned. Perhaps the woman who'd shouted at him was among them, sensing that something important had happened earlier in the evening, but unable to remember what.

Later, when the church was quite empty, Will would go to the office and take spare keys for the crypt and the side door, a more practical and speedy method than constantly relying on his powers over the inanimate. For now though, he descended to his lair, sat down in an ornate wooden throne, and started to read greedily.

Sadly, much of what Jex had written was nonsense, composed under the power of some drug or other, but in places it was quite different, almost as if written by another hand, and in those passages it took on the tone of prophesy.

Even then, little of it made sense readily, but Will pored over it, absorbing phrases and fragments—*his enemies will be legion; the circle is broken and is made complete; Asmund waits with the spirits; from four will come one; the church will speak, that has no people; the Suspended King calls across the ages.*

There was much talk of a Suspended King, a phrase he couldn't begin to understand. As of his last counting, there had been twenty-eight kings and six ruling queens in his lifetime, but he couldn't see how any of them might have been "suspended." Unless, as he hoped, this was a different kind of king; unless it spoke of and promised that second encounter with the one who had bitten him.

He turned another page and found a pencil portrait of the girl by the river. There was a beauty about her, and perhaps Jex had merely been infatuated. But after hearing him speak the way he had, it was a puzzle to find her here in this book as well as on his wall. Everything tonight had been a puzzle, a maze of words and oddities, with the girl appearing at every turn.

Will continued to leaf through the book and finally found the page that had first surprised him earlier that evening. It was all at once strange and terrifying and full of promise, a promise that this prison, its walls made of time itself, had all been for some purpose.

Was it possible he had a destiny to fulfill? For all these centuries he had considered himself cursed, a victim, and the fantasies he had entertained on and off had been of vengeance, not of fulfillment. Even now, it was the thought of a confrontation with the creature that stirred him most, but he couldn't help being drawn to the siren call of destiny, to the suggestion that his existence had meant something.

And it could not be simply the ramblings of a madman or a student of the history books because none of Will's ancestors, nor any of the usurpers of his brother's line, had ever borne his name, and so he alone knew that his name and that title had belonged together for more than seven hundred years. Nevertheless, the inscription in Jex's book was clear:

William, Earl of Mercia, will rise again.

5

One of the many mysteries that have plagued me through the years of my sickness is the question that surrounds the circumstances of my burial. By the time I first emerged from my slumber, my father and brother were already dead, the latter having lived a long and fruitful life, so there was no one from whom I might have discovered the details.

They buried me beneath the city walls. I know that much to be true. For many years I slept as my wooden casket slowly rotted and crumbled around me. It's hard for me to describe the terror I felt upon waking because I knew only one thing and knew it instantly, that I was in the grave.

I had no idea of the time that had elapsed, nor of the powers I had developed. All I knew in that moment was that I had been buried alive, and the fear and panic of that realization was like nothing I'd known before or since. My body threw itself into a terrible spasm, kicking and tearing at the crumbling walls of my coffin, so desperate was I to be free.

The first to give and break apart was on the right side, and as the soil spilled in, my violence became even more frantic. My fingernails had grown long and broke now as I scrabbled at the earth that entombed me. The hollow left by my coffin had not completely collapsed, so I was fighting through a shifting and unstable tunnel of dirt, but still I screamed and clawed like an animal in a trap. I screamed so loud, I wonder if a passerby in the world above might have heard me and feared for his life, thinking some monster or demon was about to spring forth from the earth.

At last, my hand clawed at the soil and touched stone, the foundations of the city walls, and the feel of them brought a calm over me, so powerful that I at once came back to myself. Here were the solid stones of my beloved city, and with them as a guide, I knew I could dig my way free.

I can't explain what I did next. All I can suggest is that my instinct was already reversed, that in my bones I already knew that I had more to fear from the day than from the night, from the living than from the dead.

I dug along the face of the stones, but instead of climbing upwards, I burrowed deeper until, under the wall's very foundation, the earth gave way beneath me and I fell into a small rocky chamber.

After the shock and alarm of finding myself buried, after the physical exertion of digging my way free, imagine the renewed surprise of discovering these chambers ready furnished, containing chests laden with garments and objects of use.

At first, I thought I'd stumbled into someone else's subterranean lair, and only little by little did I realize that these chambers had been prepared for me. That's the puzzle of it all—someone had known that I would be buried in that place; someone had spent considerable time and energy ensuring that I would have somewhere to live and things to live by.

The tunnel and the other chambers, the stairs to the floor of the crypt, all were much the same then as they are now. I have added furniture and comforts, most of them removed from the church above during our long shared history, but much was already there.

Yet for all the efforts that had been made on my behalf, no word had been left for me, no guide to tell me what I'd now become or how I would live, what powers were mine, what dangers lay ahead. As I look back, I can only conclude that my ignorance, too, was part of the design, that it was always intended I should find my own way.

As I bathed in my pool for the first time, I slowly began to take note of the changes that had taken place in my person. For one, the functions of my body seemed somehow suspended. I felt no hunger for food. Nor, for all my exertions in freeing myself, was there any odor about me.

My hair and nails and my canine teeth had all grown, though the rest of me remained as on the day I'd fallen sick. And then I saw the source of my sickness, the faint scars on the inside of my forearm where once there had clearly been puncture wounds, as if some animal had bitten me.

I rubbed at the wound, which was already a ghost of itself and has now long since disappeared. Then I bit lightly on the back of my hand and saw the indentations left by my own teeth. I understood immediately that I had not been bitten by an animal, but by a person, and that whatever kind of person had bitten me, so that was the kind of person I had now become.

I had been made a demon, that was how it seemed to me, and I thought back to the strange atmosphere that had pervaded the city on the night the witches burned and in the weeks building up to it. It was as if the Devil himself had walked abroad that night and taken me for one of his own.

Many centuries passed before I first saw references to my own kind. Much of the detail was wrong, and is wrong even to this day, but there could be no mistake that the superstitions and Gothic stories referred to people who had been struck down by this very same sickness.

I do not like the name *vampire*—it seems so melodramatic, so fanciful. I have long preferred the word *undead*, and have thought of myself in that way for at least two hundred years. Is it not what I am? I have been treated as someone dead—buried, my death recorded—yet here I am, still alive, suspended in time.

I am the undead Earl of Mercia. I try to live as well as I can under difficult circumstances. I didn't choose to be this way, and for most of what I can only call "my life" I considered it no more than an unfortunate accident—only now am I coming to understand that although I did not choose to be undead, I was indeed chosen.

In the time after my first awakening, I thought it would be a matter of only days or weeks before I met the demon who'd so chosen me, who'd punctured my flesh and infected me with sickness. When he did not appear, I came to believe that I was of no interest to him, that he had selected me at random, but I still lived in the hope that one day we would encounter each other.

But we didn't. The centuries progressed and I must confess I often harbored violent fantasies about this creature. I imagined countless ways in which I might repay him for the torment I have suffered.

Even now, with the promise that this was not all for nothing, that my curse has been part of some greater plan, I pray that the discomfort in my arm is a portent, telling me that I will soon meet him whose actions sentenced me to this eternal half-life.

And I think I must kill him if I am able, if for nothing else, for my honor and the honor of my family. But above all, even above the need for revenge, I wish to ask him one simple question: why? Why me? Why then? Why all of this?

6

The church was not in total darkness. There were no lights on inside, but the glow of the floodlights illuminated the stained glass of the windows and filled the interior with a grainy twilight. It looked almost as if a thin mist hung in the air.

Will crossed the nave and climbed up the small spiraling stone staircase to the caretaker's office. He took a spare key for the crypt gate and a large iron key for the side door, probably the same two keys he'd returned in 1989 before taking back to the earth again.

He slipped the keys into his pocket, descended the steps, then opened up one of the storerooms, the door to which stood nearby, almost opposite the door up into the organ loft. He took two large candles, not because he needed them just yet, but because it was better to take little and often—things were less likely to be missed that way.

He closed the door and stood for a moment, looking down the length of the nave. It was very still, the air hazy with the strange light from the windows, but there was a troubling feel about the place and Will couldn't quite work out what it was.

He heard something behind him, nothing distinct, but turned casually to look in that direction and immediately jumped in shock. One of the large candles dropped from his hand and rolled across the floor.

The woman who'd tried to throw him out earlier that day was standing just a couple of meters away, staring at him with an expression that was somehow blank and intense at the same time. But something was very wrong.

It was the same woman in almost every regard—the short gray hair, the tweed skirt and knitted sweater, the neatly laced leather shoes—but her scent was different. He could smell people the same way people could smell freshly baked bread. Earlier, this woman had been unmistakably human, but that presence had gone.

He didn't have time to react. With a sudden burst of violence, the woman jumped into the air and he felt her foot hit him square in the chest with the power of ten men. He flew backwards and knew that he would land awkwardly, but was too amazed to try to save himself—no one had ever struck him before, certainly not with a force like this.

He landed with a crunching thud on the floor, his head hitting the stone. He felt the blow without registering any pain, but it left him disorientated for a second. He'd heard the keys fall out of his pocket as he'd landed, but astonishingly, he still clutched the other candle in his hand.

Will tried to sit up, but was once more briefly shocked by the realization that he'd been kicked maybe six meters down the nave. His attacker was walking towards him with a look of violent determination.

She was almost upon him and he knew he wouldn't have time to get to his feet. Instead, he stayed on his back and curled up into a ball, springing out of it as she reached him, planting both feet into her chest, just as she had done to him.

He scrambled upright as she shot backwards, keeping his eyes on her all the time. He was unnerved, perhaps even afraid, for the first time in centuries because he didn't know what this was. The woman flew through the air, as far as he had flown himself, but he'd kicked her at a slight angle and her body smashed into one of the stone pillars, bouncing off it before hitting the floor.

At that second, in the moment of impact, something even stranger happened. Her entire body seemed to melt into itself, forming a dark void, and as it landed on the floor, it was no longer a woman, but a wiry black dog.

He recognized it immediately as one of the dogs that had slept by Jex's stove, but he no more believed the vision before him was really that dog than he believed it was the woman he'd seen earlier in the day. The dog shook itself as if pepper had been put on its nose, and transformed again, shifting through a state of liquid confusion and emerging once more as the woman.

Whatever creature this was, Will couldn't understand why it was so intent on doing him harm, nor could he imagine how to defend himself against it. For eight centuries he had been at the top of the food chain, fearing nothing, because no other living thing had ever matched his powers.

He could only assume that all these things were connected. One divine power had led him to Jex, to the notebook that might prove the key to his existence, but another had sent this demon to attack him, perhaps to destroy him. And he didn't know how to fight it.

The woman started towards him and immediately broke into a run. Will thought of the keys and scooped them up off the floor. She was almost on top of him when he clenched his hand around the larger key, the one for the side door of the church, and held it out directly in front of him like a dagger.

She leapt for him, but he stood firm, even as he felt the force of her body crashing into his hand. He heard a tearing crunch, felt the shuddering impact, and then her face stopped at arm's length from his, her expression still stubbornly blank.

He looked down. The large black key was embedded up to his knuckles in her chest. No blood came from the wound, but around it the flesh appeared to be turning fluid, just as her entire body had turned fluid after hitting the pillar a minute before.

Will looked back at her face. Slowly, her mouth opened, and then in a detached voice, like the echo of someone talking in another room, she said, "The cathedral's closed, I'm afraid. From six o'clock on winter Tuesdays."

"Who are you?"

She smiled and once more said, "The cathedral's closed, I'm afraid. From six o'clock on winter Tuesdays." But this time he could hear another voice whispering behind hers, and as she repeated the phrase yet again, he clearly made out the words, "Death to you, William of Mercia."

He didn't have the chance to ask his question again. The woman's form turned transparent, becoming some liquid element of darkness. Then, as silently as she'd first appeared, so she had gone, into the air itself, leaving the key clenched uselessly in his outstretched hand.

Will spun around, immediately fearing that this was just the prelude to yet another attack, but there was nothing, no sound, nothing in the air. Whatever had attacked him had been destabilized enough to retreat, but he had a feeling this wouldn't be the end of it.

He gathered up the dropped candle and returned quickly to his lair. Even as he sealed the chamber door with the stone, he knew that it would be no protection from whatever demon had just shown itself to him in the church above.

What defense could he have against something that had the ability to appear and disappear at will, to shift itself from one form to another, a demon that seemed to match him for strength? Its only weakness seemed to be an inability to hold its shape when a great enough violence was done to it.

He wondered, too, why it had come to him in those forms, as a busybody old woman and a wiry black dog. Was it somehow reading his mind, making itself into the people and creatures he'd encountered in the recent past? Perhaps it would come to him next as Jex or the fireman or the girl by the river.

He opened the chest that contained his library, a collection of just a hundred or so books, accumulated over the centuries, some of them taken from the library in the church above, some from the wider city. He'd read many thousands of books across the centuries, but had discarded most, even from his memory.

This chest held all those Will considered important enough to treasure. He looked at them now, heavy volumes stacked upon each other, their ancient pages and covers, vellum and hide, protected from dust and time by the chest in which they were locked away.

There were volumes in Latin and Greek, and many more in English, or rather in many varieties of English, charting the course of his language over all this time. He could still read the handwritten and illuminated English of his childhood as easily as he could read the scribblings he'd found in Jex's notebook, even though they were almost two separate languages.

The thought of the notebook made him lower the lid of the chest again. He knew there wouldn't be anything in the books of his library that would help him understand what had just happened in the church. If anything, if there were answers, they'd be found in the notebook itself because he was convinced the events were related.

He felt a slight prickling on his skin, a sixth sense telling him that the sun had broken over the horizon in the city above. He knew how differently the city looked now, but when he thought of it at dawn, he couldn't help but see the early mornings of his childhood and it filled him with a wrenching sadness, for the mother he'd never known, for the half-brother who'd overtaken him and grown old and died, for the father who'd mourned his death, for the lost world of that other England.

Will slumped into a chair with the notebook and flicked through its pages. This is what that world had become, Jex and his dogs living in a disused warehouse where once there had been fields, surrounded by light and noise and machines where once there had been tranquility.

But his mood lifted when he thought of all that had

remained the same over the centuries, the city walls, some of its buildings and streets, and above all this church, standing proud like a beacon across time. And the people themselves, some of whom might have stepped with him from his own past, stopping only for a change of clothes.

He caught a glimpse of the girl's picture and stopped, opening the notebook to look at it once more. Something about her had enchanted him and he didn't know whether it was simply her beauty, for she *was* beautiful in an unhappy way, or a deeper sense that she was a part of all of this.

He didn't entirely believe in omens and portents, but Jex had given him a strange and demented sign in the form of this book and his dying words. It implied a destiny, just as the demon above had suggested there were forces that wanted to keep him from that destiny. And if Will had understood correctly, this girl *was* a part of it, perhaps even the key. If she was the girl Jex had spoken of then Will needed her, and though she probably didn't know it, she needed him.

7

The door of the old coffee merchant's warehouse was clearly her preferred home for the night, but now that Will was looking at her again, he was less certain that she'd be willing to guide him anywhere.

The girl looked freshly unfriendly, a hostility that seemed turned inwards at the moment, but that he guessed would be redirected at anyone foolish enough to talk to her or try to befriend her.

Why was she there? he wondered, and what had happened to her that she felt it would be better to live the winter in a derelict doorway? Perhaps there was no particular reason for her unhappiness—he knew himself that sadness never needed to explain itself, and that more often than not, it arrived unannounced and uninvited.

The unfriendliness was more of a problem. Will wanted to know her name and who she was, but to do that he had to speak to her, and for all the years he had over her, he couldn't imagine what he might say that would give him any more success than he'd had the previous night.

Right now, he wasn't even on the same side of the river. He was standing watching her from the shadows of a gutted warehouse on the opposite bank. He'd been there for close to an hour and in that time she had hardly moved. She sat like someone in a trance of misery, staring out at the darkness as if she could see all her misfortunes there in front of her.

At first, Will had been hopeful that she might be waiting; even, if she didn't know it, waiting for him. And he cursed himself for not bringing the notebook, thinking he'd have been able to sway her to his cause by showing her the picture Jex had drawn.

But as the hour had crept by, he'd become less convinced of everything. He no longer believed that she'd be able to help him or that she would want to. He even began to doubt that the things written in the notebook were anything but insane ramblings brought on by some drug or other—only the attack in the church convinced him otherwise.

Even so, he was coming to the conclusion that tonight he would just say hello in passing, allowing her to become more familiar with the sight of him before trying any more meaningful conversation. Maybe it would take several days before she was ready, but what did time matter to him?

He was distracted from his thoughts by a noise coming from near the bridge and the warehouse that was in the process of being rebuilt. A group of older boys, all dressed almost entirely in bright white clothes and shoes, a strangely joyless white, were standing around as one of them attacked the scaffolding with a metal pole he'd found nearby.

The clanging of metal against metal rang out hoarsely through the night, like an alarm warning of some terrible approaching danger. The others shouted encouragement in a coarse tongue, the words of which he could hardly make out.

After a minute or so, a man came out on to one of the balconies of the building that had already been turned into living accommodation and shouted at them. They hurled abuse back at him, but started to move on. The boy with the pole swung it around above his head and threw it. The pole didn't travel far for all his efforts and fell into the river with a dull splash.

The boys continued aimlessly, jostling each other, shouting and laughing. These were the lower classes, thought Will, and there was clearly no work for them, just as there had been none for their fathers back in the 1980s, and no power of law over them either.

He glanced back at the girl and realized that the boys were heading towards her. She didn't seem concerned, and paid no attention to them as they approached, but he was suddenly desperately worried for her and found himself hoping that they'd turn before reaching her.

He saw one of them pointing between two of the warehouses and heard him say something about a fire. Will guessed he was suggesting they explore the warehouse that had burned down the night before and he was willing the rest of the gang to take the bait, but they weren't tempted and continued on their way.

The girl still didn't stir from her corner in the deep shadows of the doorway and for a moment it looked like the group of boys would pass by without even noticing her. But then the last, the one who'd expressed an interest in the fire, saw her and said something, which in turn attracted the attention of the others.

Will couldn't understand it, but he felt slightly sick as he looked on, fearing that some violence was about to be done to her. And even though, for the first minute or two, the boys appeared to keep their distance and talked to her in low voices, he knew instinctively that they were looking for sport of some kind.

Finally, it happened, though it was less of an attack than he expected, for now at least. The one who'd wielded the pole darted into the doorway and skipped back out again, laughing, holding a black bag aloft.

The girl stood up, surprisingly tall and certainly taller

than some of her tormentors, even allowing for the step on which she was standing.

"Give it back!" Her voice rang out clearly and only now did Will notice the difference between her voice and those of her attackers—she tried to cover it, but she spoke with the tone of someone who'd known privilege, who'd been educated well, brought up well, at least until whatever calamity had left her living in a doorway.

The boys were throwing the bag from one to the other, with no apparent curiosity as to what was inside it, but their mood was becoming ugly.

"Give it back," she said again.

The one holding the bag sneered. "Or what?"

Before she could answer, the tallest in the group, who was fat and red-cheeked, but without appearing jolly, said, "You should sit down." He pushed her hard in the chest and she fell backwards into the doorway, landing on her larger bag.

The boys laughed harder and seemed excited, as if they were just beginning to realize the entertainment they could have at her expense. The pole boy had the bag again and he started to unfasten it as he said, "Let's see what's in here, eh?"

Will saw no more. He walked out of the building he was in and down the side of it, away from the river. After about ten paces, he turned and ran back towards the river, leaping from the stone wharf that made its bank.

It was maybe ten meters, but he knew he could do it,

not because he'd ever jumped it before, but because he instinctively knew what his body was capable of doing. As confidently as he'd jumped a brook as a child, so he landed on the opposite bank with such ease that they didn't even hear him.

As he approached, the pole boy took a paperback book out of the black bag, looked at it dismissively, and tossed it over his shoulder. It hit the still water with a satisfying *dunk* and the gang jeered.

The ringleader was about to go back into the bag, when suddenly he spotted Will and stopped. He looked full of hate, but Will thought there was something ugly about these boys, too—their faces were pinched and spiteful, their hair short but greased flat to their heads, which in turn looked oddly shaped. They wore earrings and had tattoos on their necks and hands.

The pole boy pointed and laughed, causing the others to turn and stare at Will as he said, "It's Countess Dracula. Come to save the witch, have ya?"

It was such a strange thing to say that Will didn't know how to respond immediately. He thought of the witches burning all those years ago, knowing now that they had been nothing of the sort, merely women who had not belonged, victims of spite and greed and suspicion.

More importantly, he wondered briefly if this boy knew who he was, but he dismissed the thought quickly enough. He'd addressed Will as a woman because of his long hair, as Dracula because of the black clothes, the pale skin. These boys were cowards, he could tell, and if they'd had even the vaguest idea of who he really was, they'd have run already.

He came back to himself, remembering why he was here. He turned first to the tall, fat boy and said, "Never strike a lady again." The fat boy looked incredulous, and was still struggling to find an appropriately abusive response when Will hit him across the face with the back of his hand.

It was meant to insult rather than cause damage, but he felt something give inside the boy's cheek, possibly a tooth being dislodged, and the side of his mouth split against Will's knuckle. The blow knocked him over, and Will immediately caught the scent of blood on his own hand—he didn't need blood, and wouldn't now for some time, but the smell of it was tempting and disturbing.

The other boys bristled, but they were looking nervously at their friend who lay groaning in pain on the floor. He noticed that they'd shuffled a step away from him. They kept throwing quick, nervous glances at the pole boy, too, and it was obvious that he was their leader even though he was far from being the tallest or most physically imposing.

For his part, the pole boy appeared to be deciding what to do. He looked Will up and down and said, "So, hard man, think you can take all of us, do ya?"

Before Will could answer, he flung the bag at him with

some force. Will caught it and threw it lightly on to the step. The girl was still lying on her other bag and he wondered if she'd hit her head as she'd fallen. She was alive, he knew that much.

He turned back to the pole boy, whose face had become even more pinched and full of venom, and immediately spotted the glint of a knife blade. A true coward, thought Will.

One of the others said, "Leave it, Taz, it's not worth it."

Another joined in, the one who'd wanted to visit the scene of the fire, saying without any conviction, "Yeah, Taz-man, chill."

The fifth member of his gang didn't say anything. He was the youngest by a year or two, perhaps fourteen or fifteen. Will could sense this boy staring at his face, could sense that he alone was possessed of enough intuition to know that Will was not what he appeared to be.

Taz, for that seemed to be the pole boy's name, was having none of it. He jabbed at the air with the knife and said to Will or to the others or perhaps even himself, "I'm chilled. You want it? C'mon, Goth boy."

Will took a quick step towards him. As he did so, he noticed Taz's advisers backing away. The fat boy was still groaning on the floor and cursing about his tooth. Only the fifth boy kept his ground, staring, mesmerized.

The blade flashed again as Taz made a panicky lunge, and then he looked alarmed as he realized that

Will had caught his fist in his own hand and was now holding him firmly. His mouth looked on the verge of speaking, but Will's hand was crushing his fingers around the blade of the knife and the pressure was beginning to tell.

Will stared into his eyes, catching him with a hook that pulled him out of the world he knew. Taz could no longer see or hear his friends, no longer knew whether it was day or night or where he was. He'd lost the power to cry out, so even as the pain twisted his face, he remained mute and his tear-filled eyes never once strayed from Will.

Will tightened his grip further and felt the pressurized crack as one finger broke against the handle, then another. The noise of slowly breaking fingers was enough to send two of the gang running into the night.

He listened to their footsteps thumping away towards the background noise of the city traffic, then let go and heard the knife drop to the floor. He smiled and said softly, "Run away home, Taz, and never come back here again."

Will stood aside and watched as Taz came back to himself, as he looked down at his shattered hand and cried and stumbled forwards, breaking into a run. His fat friend shouted after him and, realizing he was being left, scrambled to his feet and lumbered off in the same direction, still cursing about his tooth.

There was a sudden movement in the doorway as

the girl came to with a start, letting out an offended, "Ow! Bloody hell!" She was holding her head with one hand, searching for her bag with the other.

But Will didn't go to her. He looked instead at the fifth member of the gang who still stood exactly where he'd been the whole time. He didn't appear afraid in any way, but nor did he seem threatening—he looked like someone who'd experienced a revelation or a religious conversion.

Without saying anything, he bent down and picked up a couple of small objects, the things Taz had discarded from the bag before Will's arrival. He walked over then and held them out. It said something for his spirit that he didn't even flinch as Will reached out and took them from him.

"Sorry about the book," said the boy. Up close, Will noticed that he had the ghost of a scar on his left cheek.

"Thank you," said Will, and the boy stroked the scar as if it bothered him, and then walked away towards the road.

He looked back several times, and when he reached the road, he stopped for a moment before raising his hand in a wave. Will raised his hand in return, and the boy disappeared into the city.

"What happened?"

Will turned to look at the girl who was sitting on the edge of the step, rubbing her head.

"I think you banged your head."

"Cute but dumb, just my luck."

"Sorry?"

"Nothing. I know I banged my head. What I mean is . . ." She sounded incredulous as she said, "Did you beat them up or something?"

"No, not really," he said, relieved that she hadn't seen most of what had happened.

"So I don't owe you anything?"

"Of course not, nor would you if I *had* fought with them." He remembered the items in his hand and held them out to her. "He took these from your bag. He took a book, too, but he threw it in the river."

One of the items was an oddly-shaped metal pendant on a leather strap, the other a piece of plastic. She looked massively relieved to see them and for the first time let her guard down, laughing as she took them from his hand.

"Thank! God! I don't know what I'd have done if I'd lost this."

He imagined she was talking about the pendant and said, "Perhaps if you wore it?"

She looked puzzled for a second, then laughed again and said, "No, not the necklace, the memory stick." She held up the piece of plastic. "It's got all my stuff on it. Seriously, my whole life is on this thing."

Will nodded, guessing that there had been an alarming technological revolution since his last period of activity. "How's your head?"

She dropped the memory stick and the pendant into her bag as she said, "I feel a bit groggy, but I think I'm okay. It'll probably hurt in the morning but . . ." She stopped abruptly and said, "Sorry, I should have said before, thanks for helping me. My name's Eloise."

Eloise—at last, someone with a name he recognized.

"You're welcome. I'm Will."

"How old are you?"

"Sixteen."

"When are you seventeen?"

"My birthday's in March," he said, carefully not answering the question.

"October, so technically, you're older than me, but girls mature quicker."

"True," he said, and left it at that. Not only was he much older than her, he was also like an insect trapped in amber. Eloise was heading towards her seventeenth birthday, eleven months from now, but his would never come. One day soon she would be a grown woman. She would marry and have a family and grow old, and he would still be the sixteen-year-old boy she saw before her right now.

"You look sad," she said.

"I am, a little, but it passes soon enough."

Eloise nodded, but then looked full of mock suspicion and teased him as she said, "Were you spying on me, Will? It's pretty convenient that you happened to come along just when I needed a rescuer."

"I did just happen to walk along at the right moment, but I was coming here to see you."

"Why?"

"I don't know. Why does anyone want to get to know someone else?"

She looked taken aback by the directness of his response, perhaps realizing that he was more mature than the average boy she encountered. She almost looked in danger of being won over, but as if remembering her former frostiness, her face hardened.

"That's a nice thought, and I'm really grateful to you for seeing off those . . ." She struggled to think of an appropriately awful word to describe them and eventually gave up. "The thing is, Will, I don't need any friends right now. I'm here because I want to be on my own. I don't want to know people."

"I understand," said Will, and took a step back, but he hadn't given up just yet. "There was something else, too. Someone who just died gave me a notebook—it had your picture in it."

Eloise looked intrigued, but not enough to be won over. Even so, she said, "Was it the *Big Issue* seller?"

"Yes, did you know him?"

She shook her head doubtfully as she said, "No, not at all really, but he was always talking to me. Like, in a creepy way. When you say a drawing?"

"Of your face. He had another on the wall of his . . ." He didn't want to say *hovel* and struggled for a second or two to remember what they'd been called in the 1980s. "His squat. I imagine that one burned in the fire."

"They think he killed himself, but I'm sure he was on drugs, so it could've been accidental, I suppose."

"You never sat for him?"

"God, no! Honestly, I didn't know him. He'd just talk to me if I saw him in the street. And he gave me that necklace, the one you just found, said it was meant to be mine or something creepy like that. You know, I think he'd spent too long in India or somewhere. If I'd known he was drawing pictures of me, I'd have been really freaked out."

"I can imagine." Will thought about it and realized she probably wasn't part of this, that it was wishful thinking to believe she was anything other than a homeless girl. And she was beautiful and pleasant to talk to, but he knew from past experience that it wasn't safe for him to have friends—perhaps even less so now. "Well, good night."

He started to walk away, but Eloise seemed to change her mind, or was at least curious, and called after him. "Will, wait there."

As he turned, she jumped up and stepped towards him, but immediately faltered, as if she'd lost her balance. She stopped and put one hand against the wall, the other on her head.

He was about to go to her aid, but she said, "I'm fine, really. I probably have a concussion or something, that's all. I just . . . you didn't explain why you wanted to talk to me about that guy . . . actually, forget that, do you think we could go and get a cup of tea or something? I'm feeling a bit shaky."

"Of course."

"Good, there's a vegan café just inside the gate that's open late. We can go there."

He nodded, but said, "What is a vegan?"

Eloise laughed. "Are you for real?"

"I beg your pardon?" Will was suddenly having trouble understanding everything she said, as if he was the one who'd been knocked unconscious.

"You don't know what a vegan is?" He shook his head. "Someone who doesn't eat any animal produce at all."

"Oh, I see, like a vegetarian. And are you a vegan?"

"No." He was disappointed somehow—he'd liked the idea of her being a vegan and him being someone who survived exclusively on the most animal product of all. "I'll just put my bag away and we'll go."

He watched as she dislodged one of the broken panels in the wooden door and pushed her larger bag through it. She picked up the other bag and said, "Okay, Will, let's go."

They started walking and as much as he knew it was a bad idea, he was happy not being alone for once. He'd almost forgotten the attack in the church the night before, the rambling prophecies in the notebook, even the very thought of having a destiny. For now, he could think only that she was almost as tall as him, that they were both dressed in black, both pale, walking as one—it was almost as if they were meant to be together.

8

They turned left inside the South Gate and then right into a narrow lane that had been blocked to cars and other vehicles, but would probably have been too narrow for them anyway. Crooked and gabled buildings hung over each side as the lane twisted its way towards the church.

They hadn't walked far up the lane when Eloise stopped and said, "This is it."

Will looked at the timber-framed building, its upper floors overhanging the lane. He remembered when it had been new, in the period after his second hibernation, more upright then, cleaner, but not much different otherwise.

It was called the Whole Earth and the wooden sign

that hung out into the street was decorated on each corner with a pentagram, the five-pointed star so loved by magicians and mystics.

"This was a tavern," he said, thinking aloud. "For a long time it was called the Green Man."

Eloise looked puzzled and said, "How do you know that?"

"My family lived around here for centuries. I suppose someone must have told me when I was younger."

She seemed satisfied and walked in ahead of him. It was past ten, but the place seemed busy. Nearly every table in the main room was occupied, mostly by people who looked like Jex or Eloise or some variation of the two of them, drinking soup or eating sandwiches made of coarse bread, sipping hot drinks in tall glass-and-metal mugs.

It was dimly lit with lamps and candles, which suited Will's eyes, and much of the decoration seemed to hint at witchcraft and magic, as well as other things that appeared to come from the Orient. He couldn't quite understand the confusion of images and what they all meant together.

Eloise led the way into one of the smaller snugs. There were only two other people in there, sitting in the corner, a woman with glasses and a man with a beard who had the scent of death about him, though Will guessed he didn't know it yet, judging by his jovial mood.

They sat in a wood-paneled alcove, with a simple black-and-white drawing in a frame on the wall, which appeared to show the seven witches on their pyre. Eloise followed his gaze and said, "I don't know how true it is, but the story goes that they brought the witches here before they were burned. I suppose that would make sense if it was a tavern."

Will looked at her, and wanted to tell her that this building had not been here then, that if it had, those poor women would hardly have been granted its comforts, but he was distracted by the sight of her face directly across the table from him. It was the first time he'd seen her close up.

Her skin appeared a little less pale now that she was indoors. Her lips were full and soft, her eyes the purest blue, a blue that reminded him of the daytime summer sky that he would never see again.

Looking into her eyes had the strange effect of filling him with longing for some half-remembered afternoon, a disjointed sense of peace that seemed lost in time. He tried to remember when that afternoon might have been, but couldn't place it, almost as if it was an afternoon he was yet to experience, as impossible as he knew that was.

"What are you looking at?"

"Sorry, I didn't mean to stare. I like your eyes."

"You can have them if you want." She responded to his confused expression by laughing and saying, "I'm joking. I don't even know what I meant by that. Thank you. And you have nice eyes, too—kind eyes."

There had been kindness in them a long time ago, perhaps, but not anymore.

He looked at her hair and said, "Your hair isn't really that color, is it?"

"I wish," she said, and ran her hand absentmindedly through it before brushing it back, almost as if about to put it into a ponytail. "It was brown, but you're right, this is dyed. Isn't yours?"

"No," he said simply.

He'd been conscious of the faint discomfort in his arm where the wound had once been, but it flared up now, intensifying so much that he wanted to scratch at it. He didn't, but only because of the way he imagined Eloise would react.

Even as he fought to resist the impulse, an attractive young woman appeared at the side of their table and smiled at Eloise. She was very thin and tanned, with blonde hair pulled back and a metal ring in her nose. She was wearing jeans and a patterned red-and-yellow T-shirt that was so small and tight it might easily have been meant for a child. Her wrists were adorned with the same array of bracelets and bangles that he'd seen on Jex.

"Hello, Ella, who's your friend?"

"Hi, Rachel, this is Will."

The woman turned and looked hard at Will, smiling all the time, then said, "Hi, Will, welcome to the Whole Earth."

"Thank you," he said, and waited for her to turn away, his old wound burning furiously. But she continued to stare at him for several seconds, trying to hide what looked like an expression of intense curiosity. It was almost as if she recognized him, and now he wondered if the flaring up of the wound could be a response to her.

"Okay, what can I get you two? Anything to eat?"

"Not for me," said Eloise. "Just some chamomile tea."

"I'll have the same, thank you."

"Coming right up," said Rachel, and walked away, the ancient floorboards creaking even under her slight frame. Will couldn't be sure if the discomfort in his arm subsided as she walked away or if he just imagined it did.

Trying to shake off his suspicions, he said, "She called you Ella."

Eloise looked around to make sure no one else was listening in, but the couple in the corner were too concerned with each other, laughing intimately.

"I didn't want people knowing my real name, just in case, you know." He nodded, assuming she meant that she was a runaway, that her family might come looking for her. As if she'd heard his thoughts, she said, "I'm an orphan, too."

"Oh, I'm sorry." Echoing her question to him the night before, he said, "Was it long ago?"

"When I was a baby—car crash. My parents, brother, and sister, all killed. I didn't get a scratch. I was too young to remember anything about it."

"How sad." Will thought of her growing up, being aware that she'd once had an entire family but never actually knowing them. "Is that why you . . . ?"

He tried to find the right words to express her current circumstances, but she got there ahead of him and said urgently, "God, no! No, I was brought up by an uncle and aunt and, you know, I was at prep school from seven. No, I haven't wanted for anything."

"So why are you living in a doorway?"

Before she could answer, Rachel returned with two mugs of chamomile tea, the clear liquid visible through the glass tumblers, which sat inside ornate metal holders. His wound didn't twinge, so maybe he *had* been imagining it.

"Two cups of chamomile tea and these are on the house."

"Thank you," they said together, Eloise sounding surprised. Rachel smiled at her, but once more, Will noticed her staring at him as she turned to walk away again, her eyes fixing on him for just a moment too long.

He knew he was striking in appearance, but he sensed there was more to it than that, even if he couldn't work out what it was exactly. Whether or not the sensation in his arm had been a response to Rachel, there was still something odd in her reaction to Will.

Eloise hadn't noticed anything and said, "Rachel and Chris are really cool. Made a load of money in the dot-com boom, did the backpacker thing for a while, bought this place. They're in their thirties, you know? Seriously, I hope I'm still that cool when I'm their age."

He'd understood only half of what she'd just told him, so he repeated his earlier question. "What happened to you? Why are you living in a doorway?"

She looked embarrassed and bit her bottom lip. "It was a mistake, something that just . . . okay, here goes. My uncle and aunt divorced when I went to prep school—they didn't have kids of their own and I think they only stayed together until I was old enough to board. I've spent holidays moving between the two of them ever since, mainly with my aunt actually, even though she isn't the blood relative. Tell me if this is boring."

"Not at all, please continue." Will had the feeling she hadn't had the opportunity to talk about this to anyone for some time and there was something soothing for him, too, in the sound of her voice, in the simple comfort of human company, of sharing space with another person.

Eloise tried to sip at her tea, but found it too hot and put the mug back down before continuing. "Anyway, this summer, neither of them were around. Uncle Matt was on business in China with his new girlfriend. Aunt Lucy was on a round-the-world cruise—I mean, how tacky is that? So I was left at Lucy's house, which is in the middle of nowhere, and I don't know anyone, except the maid who doesn't speak English. So I fell into a real slump, and then I found out that one of my supposedly best friends had invited another friend, and a boy, over to her family's place in Italy and hadn't even told me."

She paused and made a renewed attempt at the tea before she said, "Okay, that doesn't sound much, but I was feeling really sorry for myself, feeling all alone in the world, like no one would miss me, and I was hating the thought of going back to school, so I just didn't . . . go back, that is. I got the train up here and just didn't go any further. It was easy really."

"So you've been living on the streets ever since?"

The man in the corner overheard him and glanced around in concern, craning his neck to try to see who else was in the alcove. Will shot a glance back at him, disconcerting enough for the man to turn away. He almost felt like going over and telling him—*that sickliness you feel, it's in your blood and your heart, and you don't know it now, but you're already as good as dead, so dead that I wouldn't even feed on you.*

"Two months. It wasn't too bad at first, but I have to admit, now that it's getting colder . . ." She sounded distracted and then said, "If I'm honest, I feel like a fraud."

"Why?"

As if it hardly needed stating, she said, "Because I've had a privileged life, and the people who are living on the streets here and everywhere else are doing it because they've got no choice. You know, kids who've been abused, people with addictions. I mean, even those kids who were hassling me tonight, and thank you, by the way. Did I thank you for what you did?"

"You did, and I didn't do very much."

Eloise nodded, uncertain, and said, "Well, thanks again anyway. But those kids have probably had a lot less in their lives than I've had."

Will thought of them, wearing white in winter, wondering how they could dress in such a way and be as badly off as she imagined. He didn't doubt that they were from the lower ranks of society, but at first sight, their lives were clearly removed from the poor of nearly every period he'd so far witnessed.

"So if you feel like a fraud and the weather is growing too cold, why do you stay?"

Eloise looked even more embarrassed and stared at her tea for a few seconds before saying, "Partly, I suppose, because it's just so difficult to admit that it was a mistake. My latest plan is to hold out till Christmas, then go back and say I was researching a book about being a teenager living on the streets. But it sounds pretty feeble, doesn't it?"

"You're a writer?"

"I'd like to be." She pointed at his drink and said, "You haven't touched your tea."

"No, I'm not thirsty." He knew that didn't sound like much of an explanation, so he added quickly, "Perhaps you did what you did for a reason. Perhaps you've stayed for a reason—you just don't know what it is yet."

Teasing, she said, "You mean, meeting you?"

"Perhaps," he said, smiling, enjoying the fact that she would never imagine what he'd really meant by it.

"We'll see." She finished her tea and pointed at his. "Are you going to drink this?" He shook his head and she swapped the two glasses so that his was sitting in front of her. "Anyway, now that you know everything about me—what's your story? How are you an orphan? How long have you been here? Where are you staying? All the important stuff."

Before he could respond, Eloise put her finger to her lips, though she'd hardly needed to warn him someone was coming. The irritation in his arm had quite suddenly become more intense again, close to the pain he'd briefly felt on his first reading of Jex's book.

He expected to see Rachel reappear, but a young man had come into the room. He was tall and slim and tanned, with short hair that was golden and curly on the top of his head. From the look of him and the way he was dressed, Will imagined this was Chris. And if the wound on Will's arm was telling him anything, it was that Chris was more significant than Rachel in relation to Will's destiny or perhaps more dangerous.

He went to the couple in the corner first and asked them how their food had been—their response was a little too enthusiastic—then he turned and said, "Hello, Ella, nice to see you. And this is your friend Will. I'm Chris."

He looked younger than Rachel in some undefined way,

and his eyes were dark brown and full of life. He held out his hand and Will shook it, only for Chris to say, "You're cold, Will. Still, cold hands, warm heart, isn't that what they say?"

"I believe so," said Will, and Chris seemed to find the response vaguely amusing. Even so, like Rachel, his gaze lingered on Will for a little longer than was comfortable and the old wound burned in Will's flesh. Who were these people and what were they to him, friends or enemies?

Chris finally turned to Eloise and said, "I suppose you heard about Jex, you know, the guy who sold the *Big Issue*."

As Eloise made some polite response, the couple in the corner got up and left. Will heard the woman saying something about "Year 7s" and the man responding with a comment about a staff meeting. Neither of them even glanced his way, so he guessed it wasn't anything about his general appearance that was drawing the attention of Rachel and Chris. They had both definitely seen something in him, and in turn, Will sensed they were dangerous people to be around, whether they meant him harm or not.

"I don't think they're suspecting foul play or anything. Apparently he was dead before the fire took hold, but he lit the place with candles, so he could have knocked one over in his death throes, that kind of thing."

"How awful," said Eloise. "Is that what you think happened, suicide?"

Chris shrugged. "Who knows? This is a strange city.

There's a darkness about it—that's what we like about it—but the flip side of that is bad things happen, weird things."

Eloise nodded and Will couldn't quite decide whether she was genuinely in agreement or not. As if to clear up his doubts, she said, "Darkness maybe, but not evil. And you know, he was kind, but I think that Jex guy had some serious problems."

"True," said Chris. "All the same, I want you two to be careful out there. And listen, any time you want a place to get out of the cold, you're always welcome here. You don't even have to order anything, and we're not gonna bug you with questions. I just want you to know you've got a refuge if you need it."

Eloise looked touched and said, "That's so kind, thank you so much."

Chris nodded and looked at Will, who added, "Yes, that's very generous of you."

Though Will was actually thinking he wouldn't be coming back here, at least not in their lifetimes. He had no desire to return to a place in which he sensed more danger than in any of the city's darkest corners.

"You're welcome. Anyway, I'll leave you to it."

Chris nodded again, to himself, and walked away.

Eloise was left looking slightly shocked and clearly felt she had to explain Chris's generosity. "I think they were pretty close to Jex. Maybe it's making them feel protective."

"How well do you know them?"

9

"My mother died in childbirth. My father remarried, but he died a few years later."

"Is that why you ran away, your stepmother? You are a runaway, aren't you?"

"Living with my stepmother was impossible."

Will felt guilty for suggesting his stepmother had been cruel, even seven centuries after her death, because she'd been a kind and generous lady—his mother's cousin, she'd kept alive in his mind the memory of the mother he'd never known. He had no doubt, too, that she would have mourned his death no less than if it had been her own child.

"I can believe it. Everyone I know whose parents divorced ended up with terrible stepmothers. Even Uncle Matt's girlfriends are always awful. Men just seem to get it wrong every time."

Eloise turned to see if he agreed with her, and he looked at her and smiled. "I hope I won't be like that."

"I'm sure you won't," she said confidently, facing forwards again. "You could have gone to boarding school—that would've got her out of your hair most of the time. Where did you go to school anyway?"

Will was actually enjoying creating this imaginary life for himself, the life of a twenty-first century teenager, albeit one with a slightly unusual background and an unspoken aristocratic lineage.

"Nowhere you would have heard of, but boarding would have been out of the question. She'd removed me from the school within six months of my father dying, because of the fees. So I came here. I knew my grandparents had lived here and I thought I might still have relatives locally, but I haven't found anyone."

"But you obviously have somewhere to stay." He looked puzzled by her degree of certainty and she explained, saying, "Well, I'm guessing you have possessions so you must keep them somewhere, and you look pretty well-groomed, so . . ."

"Oh, I see. Yes, I'm in a squat over near the North Gate."

She didn't respond at first and he feared that *squat* was

a word people no longer used, but after a lengthy pause, she said, "You must be better at this than I am. I wouldn't even know how to go about finding a squat. As it is, if the weather turns much colder I'll have to go back whether I want to or not."

He wanted to be able to say that he'd help her, that she could come back and stay in his imaginary squat with him and his fellow runaways and travelers. He couldn't say that of course, but he couldn't help thinking she'd feel snubbed by his silence.

"Where would you go?"

"Home, I suppose, to begin with. I don't even know if the school would take me back—I haven't given it much thought."

Suddenly, he saw a way out and said, "I'd have to discuss it with the other people in the squat first, but if they were okay about it, you could come and stay there."

Eloise stopped walking and looked at him, mortified as she said, "Will, I wasn't asking to stay at your place. Honestly. God, that must have sounded awful, and really, I'd never put someone in a position like that."

"If it was my place alone, you wouldn't need to—I would have offered you shelter the moment I saw you in that doorway."

She continued to look at him, a quizzical smile spreading across her face. Finally, she said, "You know, I don't think I've ever met anyone quite like you. You're like some old-fashioned knight."

"Thank you, though it's a while since I killed a dragon."

She laughed and said, "The night isn't over yet."

Will's instinct would have been to cut in among the old warehouses, but Eloise kept to the main road until they reached the bridge, then turned left. He supposed it was the sensible thing for her to do, to keep away from the dark and deserted corners, the exact same places in which he felt safest.

As they walked past the warehouse, which had been converted, they both looked in at the rooms that were still lit, though there was less activity visible now, just people watching television, one person walking around with a telephone.

They were alongside the second warehouse, the one clad in scaffolding, when the hairs bristled on the back of Will's neck. He stopped walking and stared into the darkness of the footpath ahead of them. Eloise had been talking, but she also stopped after a couple of paces and looked back at him.

"What is it?"

He raised a finger to his lips. She smiled at first, but his expression convinced her that he was being serious and she came back and stood beside him. Something was wrong with the air down here.

Whispering this time, Eloise said, "What is it? You don't think those boys have come back?"

Will didn't know what to do. If it was what he thought, the demon presence that had attacked him in the church, he should probably leave Eloise to walk the last stretch on her own—she'd be safer away from him, safer, too, in that she wouldn't see something she wasn't meant to see.

But he couldn't be sure that the demon would leave her alone if they parted. And even if he could, what would she think of him, scaring her like this and then leaving her on her own? There was nothing for it but to walk on.

Cautiously, he started to move again and his nerves settled a little. She stayed close but, still whispering, she said, "Slightly freaking me out now, Will."

"It's probably nothing," he said. But he'd never known an atmosphere this strange, and now that he thought about it, the air had been unstable from the moment he'd killed Jex, and maybe before that. There was something ill at ease across the entire city, as if it had been cut loose from its moorings and was now adrift in the night.

And suddenly he was even more disturbed by the realization that he *had* once known an atmosphere this strange, in the weeks before the witches had burned and his sickness struck. Could it be that the same evil had returned to the city? If so, he wasn't sure that he was ready for it.

He'd wanted to meet the person who'd done this to him for so long, and had still until a few hours ago, but now he was with the girl, the prospect set his nerves on edge. She was important to him in some way and he wanted the time and space to find out why, and to know that he wasn't leading her into danger.

They reached the gap between the scaffold-clad building and the next. Will stopped again and looked up the dark lane between the two buildings, staring in the general direction of the warehouse that had burned. There was nothing at first, but then he sensed some movement in the distant shadows.

It appeared almost as if something was moving towards them, close to the wall, low to the ground, but he couldn't actually see anything. It wasn't an animal or anything solid, more like a disturbance in the air, as if the darkness was becoming liquid around some rapidly moving object.

His body tensed up violently as the realization hit home. He grabbed Eloise by the arm and shouted, "Quick!" He ran back ten paces, dragging her with him, and shouted, "Stay behind me!"

She was panicked and shouted, "Will, you're scaring me!"

He ignored her and looked around for something to defend himself with, and more importantly, something to defend her. He was still looking when he heard a growl and turned to see a black dog had emerged from the gap and was standing on the path in front of them.

It wasn't the dog he'd seen briefly in the church, but the other one he'd noticed sleeping by the stove, not as wiry, a shaggier coat. It didn't advance at first, but stood snarling at them, its eyes fixed on Will.

"It's just a dog," said Eloise nervously. "We just need to back away slowly."

Will kept staring, but from the corner of his eye spotted an orange-and-white traffic cone under the scaffolding—unfortunately there didn't seem to be anything else at hand that he could use.

"Oh my God," said Eloise, with a mixture of confusion and concern for the animal. "I think it's on fire."

Sure enough, smoke had started to rise up from the dog's matted fur as if it had been caught in a fire and was still smoldering. At the same time, its shape seemed to be becoming unstable, then all at once, it sprang forwards and simultaneously burst into flames.

Eloise screamed, and maybe said something, too, though he couldn't make out her words. The dog didn't seem in any way slowed down or harmed by the flames, but if the plan had been to strike terror into Will, this demon had found his weakness. Fire.

He jumped urgently towards the traffic cone, picked it up with one hand, and started to turn back. He was so overcome with fear of the flames that he felt as if he was moving through molten lead, that he was too slow, that the dog would be upon him before he was able to do anything.

Even if he'd imagined his slowness, the dog had moved with terrifying speed and as he turned to face it, the animal was only meters away. It leapt towards Will and he threw the traffic cone as hard as he could. It thumped into the dog, which had managed to get close enough for him to feel the heat of the fire that engulfed it.

The dog flew backwards, maybe six meters, the fireball briefly extinguishing itself as the animal landed with a flailing crunch on the footpath. It skidded on a bit further and its shape shifted violently as it tumbled, looking for a second or two like a human form before it solidified once more into a dog.

No sooner had it regained its shape than it started running back towards him, the flames sweeping around it, then a ball of flame, hurtling along the path towards him. Without even thinking, Will reached up and tore the nearest vertical scaffolding pole from its brackets, the metal bolts shearing and flying away.

He turned, simultaneously raising the pole over his head with both hands, holding it like a lance. And this time, as the burning dog leapt towards him, he struck hard, stabbing the scaffolding pole into the heart of the flames, pinning the creature to the floor.

It writhed viciously around the pole, the fire still licking out menacingly, but Will could see it disintegrating, too, turning liquid just as the woman had in the church, almost as if the entire mass of it was being sucked back into the air.

Then as suddenly as it had appeared, the flames were extinguished and he was pressing the pole into the hard ground with no sign of the creature that had been pinned there. He kept his position, and even when he sensed it had gone, he put the pole down only reluctantly.

He turned to look at Eloise, but she was staring in

silence at the place on the path where the dog had been. She stared so intently that Will had to double-check that there was no longer anything there. He didn't know what to say to her.

The wind picked up, a gust reverberating around the warehouses. And on the back of that wind he heard a voice, an already familiar whisper, the words faint but recognizable—*Death to you, William of Mercia.* There was another noise, too, a creaking, but it was only when Eloise came back to herself and stared up at the building that he realized what it was.

The scaffolding. He grabbed her by the arm for the second time, but she knew what was happening now and ran without needing to be dragged. He heard the destabilized scaffolding straining against itself, creaking and wrenching, and they were still running when it collapsed and crashed explosively behind them.

They stopped to look. A cloud of dust was billowing up into the night sky. Much of the wood and metal had tumbled into the river and looked now like some strange playground. A couple of people walking across the road bridge stopped to stare in amazement.

"I don't understand," said Eloise. Then she looked accusingly at Will and said, "What the hell happened?"

"It must have been me—I made it unstable by pulling that pole off like that, then the wind . . ."

She threw her bag onto the floor and screamed, "No! I mean, what happened! That dog was on fire and it disappeared and what did you do? How did you break that pole loose? What! Happened!?"

He put his hands on her shoulders and stared into her eyes, but couldn't quite capture her. Having to fall back on words alone, he said, "Eloise, I'll explain everything, but right now, we have to get your other bag and we have to get out of here. The police will come."

She shook her head, making clear that he just didn't get it, and said, "I don't care about the police. I don't care about the scaffolding. I care about the monster dog that just attacked us, that spontaneously set on fire, that disappeared when you killed it."

"I don't think I killed it. I don't think it was even alive. And it wasn't attacking us, it was attacking me."

"Oh, fine. Well, that makes me feel a lot better!" Still with a tone of accusation, she said firmly, "Who are you, Will?"

"I'll tell you everything, but first we have to get away from here."

Eloise shook her head again, a little too vigorously, and he realized she was still in shock, as he supposed any normal person would have been. "Why on earth would I go anywhere with you? I've got nothing to fear from the police."

"It's your choice." He thought about it, wondering what was best for both of them. And even if she unknowingly had some part to play in whatever was now happening to him, the best thing he could do for Eloise was to leave her right there. "Actually, you *should* stay, but I have to go. Please forgive me—I didn't mean for you to see any of this and I shouldn't have let you. I'm sorry."

She nodded sadly, even though she looked as if she hadn't understood a word of what he'd said. He picked up her bag and handed it to her, and without saying anything, he walked away.

"Will?" He turned. "I'm safe, aren't I? That thing, it won't come back."

"No, it won't. You're safer away from me."

"Who are you?"

"I can't tell you, not unless you come with me."

She stared back at him, and he knew they didn't have very long, that he had to get away from there quickly. But he didn't rush her because he knew that she'd seen things she should never have witnessed, and that right now, she was making the biggest decision she would ever make.

10

Don't think I have not wished for a companion through the unending ages of my life. I have so much wanted someone to talk to, someone who would not outgrow me, and whom I would not outlive. And I have tried, but even those humble efforts met with tragedy.

I did not know it as I scrabbled through the earth from my rotten coffin, as I tumbled into the chambers that have been my refuge ever since, as I came to understand the physical changes that had accompanied my strange preservation, but the year was 1349.

Thirteen forty-nine in the year of Our Lord,

though Our Lord was not much in evidence at that time. It was a century of famine and war and revolt, and above all, it was a century of pestilence. The famine had been and gone whilst I was still in the grave, as had my father in the winter of 1263, and my half-brother early in 1320.

I knew none of this. I knew none of the history that had elapsed. I knew nothing of what I now was. If I had risen again in a time of happiness, a time of prosperity, I suspect I might well have perished before learning how I could survive alongside those who still lived by day, but I arose in the autumn of 1349 and ventured out into my beloved city in the nights after the plague had arrived at its gates.

I have often wondered since if it was the very stench of the Black Death that had roused me in the first place. When I first saw the panic that filled the city, the corpses that fell almost too quickly to be buried, the stench, and the squalor, I couldn't help but connect it all with the burning witches, as if their execution had set the world upside down.

Little did I realize that life had returned to normal after that awful night, that good seasons and bad had come and gone in the years since. The world had not ended in October 1256—it just appeared that way to me.

Given how inexperienced I was in procuring the blood I needed, given that I only understood that need little by little, the plague became my friend, bringing mayhem and fear to the city in order that I might walk through it unnoticed.

In the midst of all that horror, my torn and bloodless victims aroused no great suspicion—as far as the people were concerned, the Devil was at work across the entire land—and anyway, the plague left its corpses even more disfigured than I left mine. All were buried together, most without ceremony.

Did I fear the plague myself? No, I did not, even before I knew that it would leave no mark upon me, for what did I have to fear from death? Yet I could smell the plague, not in the air, but in its victims, and I chose my own prey only among the healthy.

I didn't understand why. Only now do I know that what I require from the living is life itself, and that there is little to gain from a life that is already on the wane. I understand now, but back then I was driven by instinct alone, and my confusion was as great as that which reigned across the whole of Europe.

The plague receded the following year, but worse was to come in the decades that followed. The pestilence returned in 1361, in '69, in '78, and '90, and each of these successive plagues struck the young most of all, children and adolescents, sometimes singling out boys, sometimes the wealthy.

Can you understand what it was like to be trapped

forever in the body of a sixteen-year-old boy, uncorrupted by time, and over those fifty years to watch the youth of the land struck down, one generation after the other? It was after witnessing all of that death that I tried to make myself a companion.

In the winter of 1394 I befriended a servant girl. She appeared about my own age, though naturally not so tall, and I would find her most evenings in the stables, settling the horses, taking good care of them. Her name was Kate and she was my physical opposite, sandy-haired and wide-faced, her cheeks ruddy and healthy.

She knew from the start that I was high born, but she also knew her own place and never asked me more than my name. At that time, I still wore my teeth long, but she did not comment upon my appearance nor the fact that I walked only at night. Yet for all that, there was nothing simple or even retiring about her.

Each evening, I would ask her about the latest happenings in the city and she would tell me the news, of building works and trade, of crime, deaths and disputes, of the current Earl and his family—the great-great-grandson of my brother, fifth in a line of unwitting usurpers.

She had the power to amuse, too, and when she realized that I did not object to the mockery of my social equals, she became even more relaxed in my company. It may not sound a great deal, but I had known no greater friend and would wait countless lifetimes for another such.

Kate was an orphan, her parents and four brothers struck down by the last swipe of the plague's cruel hand in 1390. So when she told me that there were rumors the pestilence had once again returned to London—rumors that eventually proved unfounded— I became concerned that she would meet the same unhappy fate as her family.

It seemed so very simple. I knew where I had been bitten and reasoned that if I bit Kate on the arm, if I drew blood, but not enough to kill her, then she, too, would become like me. She would be saved from the pestilence forever, and I would no longer be alone.

It makes it no easier to bear that Kate offered me her arm willingly, that she trusted me so much or valued her future so little that she was happy to risk her life on my promises.

I wonder if she had fallen in love with me or if I had unwittingly mesmerized her, a process I still did not fully understand at that time. I'm pained to think that her decision might have been unduly influenced, that she might not have fully understood what I was asking of her.

I drew almost no blood at all from the wound and she did not complain or cry out, but within an hour, she had fallen into a sleeping sickness. Still, I hoped, and carried her body away with me, and when the life was gone from her, I buried her in the earth in my own chambers.

I waited sixteen years, and when I finally dug in that spot and found her bones, the rags of her simple dress, the pitiful remnants of hair, I was overcome with remorse. I burrowed like a wild animal into the soil that filled my own stone casket and I prayed that if there was a God above, He would allow me to rot also.

And as I lay there, sleep finally overcame me. I thought my wish was being granted, that death had finally come to claim me. The year was 1410 and I did not emerge again until twenty-five years later, in the long reign of Henry VI.

Had Kate not died at my hands, she would most probably have been dead by then anyway, but her loss was still a fresh wound in my mind, no less than if she had died only the night before. And it was not merely the loss of Kate that filled me with despair, but the realization that I could never have a companion, that there would never be someone with whom I could share the endless years of my existence.

Time would pass and I would forget and be tempted again by human company, and it took me hundreds of years to understand that there was nothing to gain from it, only loss for me, and danger for those who came too close.

11

Eloise insisted on carrying her own bags. The large one was a backpack, but even though she lumbered awkwardly under its weight, she refused his assistance.

They entered through the South Gate, but Will put on his dark glasses and stayed on the busiest of the roads, partly for her sense of safety, partly to avoid passing the Whole Earth again.

When she saw that he was wearing the sunglasses, she said mockingly, "Nice! You do know it's the middle of the night. You look like a complete . . ."

"I have an eye condition. The light troubles me."

"Oh, I'm sorry," she said, temporarily forgetting her

anger and fear. As if reminding herself that she had nothing to apologize for, she asked tetchily, "Where are we going anyway? To your squat, I suppose?"

"There is no squat. We're going to church."

She stopped suddenly, so fast that he'd walked a couple of paces before realizing she was no longer with him. He turned and walked back to her and she said with a hint of alarm in her voice, "You're not a born-again Christian, are you?"

He didn't know what a born-again Christian was, but he said, "No, I don't think so. I was born a Christian, but I . . ." He tried to think of words that would sum up his fall from grace, but instead, he became puzzled by the tone of her question and asked, "Is a born-again Christian more disturbing to you than what we've just seen?"

Eloise clearly thought it was a rhetorical question because she said, "Point taken," and started walking again. "It's not like I'm anti-Christian or anything. I even go at Christmas. It's just the born-again variety—I find them a bit freaky."

He couldn't help but smile to himself. He still didn't have the first notion of what a born-again Christian was and didn't want to ask, but he doubted that it could be any more freakish than him. And in turn, that thought dragged the smile from his face because it reminded him that he had disturbing things to tell her. Nor was he entirely certain of how he could make this end well.

The floodlit spire was looming ahead of them in the night sky, and as he took a left turn, Eloise realized precisely where they were heading and asked as casually as she could manage, "When you say we're going to church, do you mean we're going to the cathedral?"

"Yes," he said. "I still think of it as a church, but you're right, it's always been a cathedral."

"But it'll be closed," she protested, still apparently struggling to see that none of the rules of her world applied any more. She had just seen him fight off a demon, using powers that few humans could call upon, yet she still thought a CLOSED sign would be a barrier to him.

"I have a key."

"Of course you do," she replied sarcastically. "Because what, you do a lot of voluntary work in your spare time?"

He smiled at her, an attempt at reassurance as he said, "Because it's where I live."

Eloise didn't respond, but carried on walking with him, which was promising in itself. He led her around the far side of the church to the small side door. He couldn't see anyone about, but he walked casually and pulled her into the porch at the last possible second.

He opened the door, ushered her inside, then locked it behind them and removed his glasses. As with the previous night, the church was filled with the filtered light from the windows, but there was nothing unusual in the air now, reassuring him that for the time being, nothing awaited him there.

Eloise stopped and looked around and was briefly so overcome with the church's late-night beauty that she forgot where she was and what had happened, saying simply, "Wow, this is so beautiful. They should open it to the public at this time of night."

Will looked around, as if with her eyes, seeing the faint shafts of light with the dust dancing within them, the illusion of mist clinging to the pillars, and the distant vaulted roof of the nave. He'd seen it so many times, he'd almost lost the ability to appreciate its beauty.

Yet it was beautiful, and for him it was also home and certainty, a steady rock of the past to which he was forever fastened. No matter what the changes, this church remained, tying him and the city and the country beyond to the long history they all shared.

"This way."

He took her to the top of the steps that led down to the crypt, but she hesitated there and said, "Where are we going?"

"To the crypt. There's something I have to show you."

Still she hesitated, and as she looked down the steps, she said, "I don't know about that. It's pretty dark down there."

"Of course, I'm sorry. Please, wait here." He'd forgotten that her eyes were no more accustomed to the dark than his ever were to the light. He went away and came back with a large candle and matches, but waited until he'd started down the steps before lighting it.

She followed uncertainly and said, "I'd still be happier if we could turn on a light."

"We will, but we'll need the candle, too."

Before opening the gate into the crypt, he found the switch and turned on the lights, which were bright enough that he had to struggle not to put his glasses back on. He resisted though, and blew out the candle before opening the gate.

Eloise was more relaxed with the light on, but she still had the air about her of someone who wanted to get on with whatever it was they were doing and leave immediately afterwards. He would have to be careful how he revealed the truths he had to tell her.

He beckoned her on through the crypt and then said, "Here we are. You should take off your backpack."

She looked around, as if trying to work out what they had come to see, but took off the backpack as he'd suggested and propped it against one of the tombs.

"That tomb," he said, "the one that you've rested your bag against."

She turned. "What of it?"

"It belongs to the third Earl of Mercia, born in 1218, died in 1263. He inherited the Earldom from his grandfather, his own father having died in a riding accident."

"That's . . . fascinating."

"The tomb on your right belongs to the fourth Earl, Edward, born in 1246 to the third Earl's second wife. He lived a long life and died in 1320."

"Seventy-four," said Eloise, playing along. "I suppose that wasn't bad for those days."

"Seventy-three, but you're correct, it was a good span in such a trying age, and in truth, he should never have been the Earl at all. His half-brother, William, was born in March 1240, but fell sick in 1256, at the age of sixteen. They believed him dead, and so he never inherited the Earldom that was rightly his. But his sickness did not kill him."

All at once, Eloise understood the nature of his story, but also looked totally disbelieving. She shook her head as she said, "Now, just hold on a minute. I'll be the first to admit that something very weird happened down by the river, weird like stuff you see on television, and I'd really like an explanation. But if you're trying to tell me that you're descended from this William who was sick but didn't die, well, just forget about it because I don't believe it."

"I'm not telling you I'm descended from him."

She breathed out heavily and said, "That's a relief."

"I'm telling you I am him."

She laughed uncontrollably, a laugh that had no humor in it, and said a little too loudly, "Just! Stop! I've had the strangest evening of my life and I just need you to tell me the truth."

"But I am telling you the truth. It happened in 1256." He tried to think of how he might convince her and thought suddenly of the Whole Earth and said, "How do you think I knew that café used to be a tavern? And the burning of the witches was the night I fell sick. And how would I know so much about my father and brother?"

"I know a lot about Hitler and Stalin, but it doesn't mean I'm related to them." She reached down and picked up her bag. "I'm leaving, and if you try to stop me, I'll scream. I banged my head earlier, I must have concussion, and you . . ." She suddenly looked suspicious and said, "Did you put anything in that tea?"

"I beg your pardon?"

"You put something in the tea! That's why you didn't drink it—what did you put in it?"

Eloise was already backing away from him as he said, "I didn't put anything in your tea." She heaved her backpack up on to her shoulder and slipped her arm through the strap. "Wait. I'll give you two pieces of proof, and if that doesn't satisfy you, then fine, you can go."

"I can go if I want to anyway," she said defiantly.

"Of course, but two things first." He gestured with his hand and she reluctantly took the backpack from her shoulder again, resting it this time against the tomb of the fifth Earl, a half-nephew he'd never known. "I told you I live here, that I've lived here for nearly eight hundred years. How about if I show you where?"

Without giving her time to answer, Will knelt down and reached between the two tombs. In the dark recesses against the back wall he slipped his fingers into the small gaps and pulled the slab up. Then, once it was standing clear of the hole, he lifted it out and placed it upright on the floor of the crypt.

The slab was several centimeters thick, and he could see what was in her mind. She was thinking about the ease with which he'd lifted it, and wondering perhaps if it was even real stone. He ignored that question for now and pointed at the hole that he'd just exposed between the tombs of his father and brother.

Eloise stepped forwards cautiously. He could tell that she was nervous of getting between him and the hole, no doubt worrying that he would push her into it. He stepped back accordingly and she peered down into the dark without ever getting too close to the edge.

"That could be a priest-hole or anything," she said, though he was certain she could see the top of the steps, and that she therefore knew it was a more ambitious construction.

"True, but in fact it leads deep underground. My chambers are beneath the city walls."

Her eyes blanked him out once more and he realized that she was swayed by the things she could see, but that every time he gave her more information, she became disbelieving all over again. He decided to move on quickly.

"Second piece of proof. Why don't you see if you can lift that slab?"

Eloise looked at it and made a half-hearted effort to move it before saying, "Yeah, it's heavy, fair enough. Just like you pulled that scaffolding apart. For all I know, you could be on that drug. What is it? PCP or something."

Will picked up the stone and raised it above his head, lowered his arms so that he held the stone in front of him, raised it above his head again, and then put it back on the floor.

She looked irritated somehow and said scathingly, "So you're strong, like I'd be impressed by that."

"That isn't the proof." He grabbed her hand, and even though she looked terrified and tried to pull it away, he pressed her fingers against the side of his neck.

"Stop it! You're hurting me!"

He stared back at her and said quietly, "No pulse. I just lifted a block of stone above my head. Can you feel a pulse?"

He felt her hand relax and took his own hand away. Eloise kept her fingers pressed against the side of his neck then, confused, moved them around, prodding the flesh, searching for the pulse that he knew she would not find there.

Finally, her hand dropped to her side and she took a small step backwards. She tried to say something, but the words were lost somewhere between her thoughts and her lips. She looked down at the stone, the black hole that he'd revealed in the floor, then back at him.

And without any more warning than that, she fainted. Will leapt forwards quickly and caught her before she hit the stone floor, which was just as well because he didn't want her banging her head for a second time in one night.

He lowered her gently to the floor before looking around and thinking through the logistics of moving her.

He'd been concerned about how he would persuade her to follow him underground, but now at least that problem had been solved—he'd carry her. He only hoped that when she awoke, she'd remember why she'd fainted in the first place, and that the memory of it would prepare her for the equally extraordinary things he still had to tell her.

12

Will sat in his chair, close to the daybed on which Eloise now lay. It was late and he guessed that tiredness had overtaken her just as much as the shock of the things she'd seen and experienced. Her sleep had been troubled to begin with, but now she was lying peacefully, facing him.

He sat looking at her, at the gentle landscape of her black-clothed body, at the pale beauty of her face, the soft pink of her lips. And he wished more than ever before that he could be fully human again, even for the simple pleasure of lying there with her, of falling into a human sleep, of waking with her in his arms.

These were childish dreams, of pleasures that would never be his. Nor did he need to remind himself of that because there was still the distant, dull ache in his arm, declaring what he truly was.

It was almost as if the creature who made him was calling to him from far away, reminding Will that he hadn't finished with him. It troubled him more now, knowing that he might well be leading this girl into danger, but unable to stop himself.

He rubbed idly at his arm, as if that could rid him of a discomfort that was in his soul, and without warning, he found himself dreaming. It happened rarely, and they were visions rather than dreams—a part of him was still conscious of the room about him, of its sounds and scents, and he wasn't sleeping because he didn't sleep outside the long, black nights of his hibernations.

It was like a dream though, one from which he didn't want to wake, inspired no doubt by the sight in front of him. Because he was walking among the ruins of an ancient building in the countryside. It was a summer afternoon, like the afternoons of his memory, a warm, blue sky dotted with harmless clouds, and he was walking with her, with Eloise.

Neither of them was talking. They simply walked together among the fallen stone walls, and when she turned to face him, she smiled and he was stunned by her beauty, and saddened in the knowledge that this day could never be, in more ways than one.

Then, as if a cloud had covered the sun, her smile fell away and Will became uneasy. He didn't want her to speak now, but she did and her voice was full of sadness as she said, "Will you sacrifice me, when the time comes?"

"No," he said, aware that he'd spoken aloud rather than within the vision, but even as the dream shattered and left him stranded back in his dark chambers, he saw in the last glimpse of her face that she didn't believe him.

He looked at the daybed and, as if woken by his voice, Eloise stirred and lifted her face to look at him. It had been a dream, nothing more, but Will almost wanted to tell her again, the real Eloise, that he wouldn't let any harm come to her.

She stared at him for a second or two before cautiously pushing herself upright and leaning back against the wall. He'd been careful to light candles here and there so that she wouldn't be too disturbed upon waking. Even so, her surroundings were still something of a shock to her.

She looked around the chamber, glancing at the wooden chests, the bare stone of the walls, the dark openings into the other anterooms. With the exception of the bed and two padded wooden thrones, the candlesticks, and chests, there was no other furniture and no other decoration.

He needed nothing else, and everything was stored in such a way that it would survive intact through the years of his hibernations, hence the wooden chests rather than anything more homely. But he could see how, to her, or to any normal living person, this would seem an unfriendly place, perhaps even the Gothic lair so beloved of storybook vampires.

"Where am I?"

"This is my . . . my home." He could tell that she was remembering, the stone lifted from the floor of the crypt, the steps descending into the darkness. "It's safe. The city walls are directly above us."

She glanced up at the roof of the chamber.

"You didn't put anything in my drink." It wasn't a question this time, but a realization that none of this had been imagined or hallucinated.

"No."

"Who are you?"

"I am William, the rightful Earl of Mercia. I was born in 1240, struck down by sickness in 1256 and I have been like this ever since."

"I know, you told me all that." Eloise struggled to put her thoughts in order and said, "Okay, what I mean is, *what* are you? You're not a ghost." Before he could reply, an answer sprang into her head and, as if it should have been obvious from the start, she said, "You hypnotized me! You're like that guy off the TV—you do all this mind control . . . You hypnotized me, to make me believe all this is real."

He shook his head gently, but instead of answering her directly, he said, "For a long time I had barely an idea of what I was myself. I knew only that I'd been buried alive, that when I stirred, nearly a hundred years had elapsed and yet my body was not a day older. I knew I had been bitten, I knew I needed blood, but in more than seven hundred and fifty years I have never met another like me or been given any guidance or explanation. Only halfway through that span did I first hear tales of beings that shared my habits, and only in the last two hundred years have I read enough to be certain that these stories refer to people like me."

"Oh. My. God. This is amazing," Eloise said, and stared at him with her eyes so wide open that he became concerned she might be once again about to faint. But she sounded almost playful as she said, "You're a vampire!"

"I prefer the term undead."

As if she hadn't heard him, she was still teasing, even suggestive, as she said, "Are you going to suck my blood?"

"Never," he said, even though under different circumstances she would have made an ideal victim—unloved, unmissed, alone.

But Eloise appeared bizarrely unconcerned. She glanced around, saw her small black bag next to the bed, and reached down for it. She rooted around before pulling something out and turning to face the wall. It was a small mirror, the glint of the candles shining back at him.

"I can see your reflection."

"Nor am I afraid of garlic, though I find its scent off-putting, and as you can see, I live beneath a church so, far from filling me with terror, the crucifix is a symbol of my one true refuge from the world. I can't help the superstitions and the folklore. I can only tell you what I see of myself, and what I know to be true."

"Fire," she said, perhaps thinking back to the blazing dog.

"Yes, and light, sunlight most of all. A stake through the heart will weaken me, and incapacitate me for some time, but it won't kill me."

Intrigued, she asked, "How do you know?" He opened his shirt and pointed to the faint scar in the middle of his alabaster-white chest. Amazed, she said, "Someone put a stake through your heart?"

"That's a story for another time. Anyway, it was a long time ago."

"Show me your teeth."

"I file them," he said as he moved closer and opened his mouth.

"Gross, why would you want to do that?"

"It's easier and cleaner to use a knife; it leaves a suicide, not a corpse with puncture wounds. It makes my appearance less conspicuous. I need to be able to walk among people without standing out."

Eloise swung her feet around and sat on the edge of the bed. Far from being terrified or disbelieving, she now seemed excited by what he was telling her, as if she'd been waiting to encounter someone like him her whole life.

Little did she know either that his hopes rested on the

possibility that she *had* been waiting for this meeting from the day of her birth, that it had been planned by fate and that she had a specific part to play in his destiny. He hoped for both their sakes that their meeting had not been an accident.

"So how does this work? You rise by night and sleep by day, though I'm guessing it's not in a coffin, right?"

He was thrown by the lightness of her tone, by her apparently genuine interest in something that should have filled her with horror.

"I rest during the day, but I don't sleep. I hibernate for long periods, years or even decades, in there." He pointed to the other chamber.

"How often? I mean, when did you last hibernate?"

"Nineteen eighty-nine."

At last, her thoughts stumbled, and after looking perplexed for a moment, she said, "Okay, so you're sixteen, but you hibernated before I was born and emerged again . . . when?"

"Yesterday, shortly before meeting you."

She took in the information and said, "So you would have needed blood." Her tumbling thoughts gelled into a sudden, awful clarity and she blurted out, "You killed Jex!"

"Who gave you the creeps, whose name you didn't even know."

"True, but even so, you killed someone yesterday. Have you killed anyone today?"

He shook his head. "I need to feed when I emerge from hibernation, but after that I need it rarely. I think it depends on the person, on how much life there is in them."

Eloise was insistent, saying, "About how often, on average?"

"It's impossible for me to say. Sometimes as much as a year, more commonly it's measured in months, sometimes even less."

"So you might have to kill someone else before Christmas, or you might not, all depending on how good Jex's blood was." Her tone sounded light at first, but it was laced with a hint of anger, or at least outrage.

"I've killed hundreds of people because it's what I need to do to survive; it's what I am. But you have to understand something else: I've seen millions die, and I will see millions more. In that regard, death is all I know." She looked ready to respond, but he cut her off as he said, "Even you. Here we are today: in appearance we're the same age, but you'll grow up and grow old and die, as everyone you know will die, including your children, grandchildren, and their grandchildren, and through all those lifetimes I will remain as you see me now. You understand? Death is the backdrop against which I act out my life."

She didn't respond at first, but looked around the chamber again and said, "Did you do all of this or was it already here?"

"It was prepared for me."

"By . . . ?"

"I wish I knew. I've always presumed it was the one who bit me, but I don't know, and have never met that person." He'd never met him, that was true, but he felt uncomfortable not telling her the whole truth of what he suspected was happening now. He could see Eloise's next question forming and jumped in first, adding, "And no, I don't remember being bitten."

"But that suggests you weren't just bitten by accident, doesn't it? Surely it suggests you were bitten for a reason."

"It does, but for the better part of a thousand years there hasn't been any indication of what that reason might be, until now."

Jumping ahead, she said, "You think it's something to do with me, don't you?" She seemed excited and didn't wait for an answer. She leapt from the daybed and knelt in front of him, holding on to his arm. "Will, make me a vampire—make me like you."

He was shocked, hardly believing he'd heard her correctly. He stared deep into her eyes and he could see that she wanted this, but that she hadn't even begun to understand what "this" was. Her own life seemed bleak to her right now, bleaker than he'd imagined, but this would be no solution, even if it were something he had within his power.

He put his hand on hers and said, "I tried once before, when I was much younger." Her eyes looked full of hope, and he was transfixed by them, a blue he could easily imagine himself staring into for another thousand years, even as he knew it wasn't to be. "It didn't work. She died, but if I'd understood the curse I would have been inflicting, I wouldn't have done it anyway."

Eloise looked deflated, and he could tell that part of her didn't believe him, a part of her that thought he was simply testing her determination. "You don't understand, it wouldn't be a curse, and we'd have each other as company, and I wouldn't be losing anything."

By her own admission, she'd led a privileged existence, albeit one devoid of love, so he could only assume she was being reckless, that she didn't even understand what she was asking of him. Kate's had been a reasonable gamble, but he couldn't believe Eloise's life was empty enough to make his existence seem attractive to her.

"Eloise, you won't be sixteen forever. Even if I could, I wouldn't deny you that." He saw that she was ready to argue again, so he added quickly, "Besides, if I'm right, I think I need you, and I need you alive."

It seemed to do the trick and she was sidetracked enough to ask, "Is this because of Jex's notebook?"

"Yes, it is."

She nodded in resignation, and looked on the verge of speaking again, but she was stopped short by a dull clanging noise, the sound of metal hitting stone. They both looked at the stone blocking the entrance to his chambers because the noise had come from the other side of it.

Eloise whispered, "Someone must have followed us."

Will shook his head as they both stood. He knew they hadn't been followed, just as he knew that the tunnel from crypt to chamber led nowhere else and that no one but him had been there in nearly seven hundred years.

The noise sounded again, the metal pounding against the outside of the stone as if someone was trying to smash through. Will moved silently over to the largest chest and opened it. He drew the sword from a sheath that lay diagonally down the side of the chest.

He didn't know if the sword would be any use, but he wanted to be armed, particularly after the attack by the burning dog—even the thought of fire was enough to send a ripple of fear through him. He didn't know what was beyond the stone door, whether spirit or demon, but he was certain of one thing, it wasn't human.

"Who do you think it is?"

He shrugged and said, "A demon attacked me in the church last night, in the guise of a woman who'd tried to throw me out. It attacked me again tonight in the form of Jex's dog. I fear this is another such assault."

He didn't bother telling her that the attacks were becoming more frequent, probing his weaknesses, and that he needed to find a way of putting a stop to them soon.

"And does this happen a lot?" Eloise sounded as if she needed reassurance, as if this was something he was quite used to.

But he shook his head. "As I said before, everything seems different this time—Jex, you, this demon."

"But surely it can't get in? That stone looks . . ."

As if in response, the stone shuddered as it was hit with another clang, the sound hovering this time like the ringing of a cracked bell. Rubble clattered down on the other side of it. Will turned to Eloise and gestured with his hand for her to stay where she was.

She backed against the wall and said, "You're not going to open it!"

"It's always better to face danger head on." He was sounding braver than he felt because he had no idea who or what was outside. Even so, he slid the sword through his belt and lifted the huge stone to one side.

He stepped back, drawing his sword again and preparing for an attack, hoping only that he would be able to fend it off. He sensed the distortion in the air immediately, and yet he was still shocked when the person on the other side stepped calmly into the chamber.

Will heard Eloise gasp, and then with a mixture of shock and suspicion, she said, "I don't . . . I don't understand. What the hell's *he* doing here?"

13

Taz! There he stood, the ringleader of the boys who'd harassed Eloise by the river, his clothes still dazzling white, a metal pole held casually at his side.

He looked real enough, his face full of the same mean hatred, but this was no living boy. He stared at Will blankly and spoke in a voice that was distant. "You want it? Come on, Goth boy!"

Will didn't have time to respond. Taz swung the pole fiercely towards his head. Will raised his sword in a reflexive defence, but moved away from the force of the blow at the same time.

Pole hit sword, sending sparks skittering across the

gloomy chamber. As if he'd used such a weapon his whole life, Taz immediately swung a second blow, this one shuddering through the blade of the sword, convulsing violently up his arm and into his body.

Another two blows followed quickly afterwards, both so powerful that Will feared the blade of his sword would shatter under the impact. He hadn't used a sword since the sixteenth century and the shock of the attack was leaving him with little choice but to fight defensively.

But as he fought off the blows, he kept reading his opponent's movements. He was impressed, thinking that in many ways Taz fought in much the same way he did—he was even a fellow left-hander. But that in turn made Will realize that Taz also shared some of his weaknesses, and in particular, a tendency to fight high and leave his underbelly exposed.

Thwack! The next crashing blow came in, then another, but this time, as the metal pole swiped through the air towards him, Will dropped to the floor and immediately lunged forwards, thrusting the blade of his sword up towards Taz's chest.

But he stopped short of pushing the sword in. Just in time, he remembered that the demon had disappeared each time he'd stabbed it, first with the key, then with the scaffolding pole, and he didn't want it to disappear. It wasn't enough to destroy each demon—he had to find out why they were attacking him. So he pressed the sword firmly against Taz's chest, but didn't break the surface.

Taz stopped abruptly and dropped the metal pole on the floor. He looked down at the point of the sword on his chest, then up at Will. He jumped backwards from the blade then, and before Will could respond, he turned and ran into the passage.

Will started after him, but was stopped when Eloise called out, "Will?"

He looked back at her. "This demon, it's feeding off me in some way, off the things I've seen. It even fights just like me. I have to find out why."

He ran into the passageway as Eloise said, "I'm coming with you." And he could hear her footsteps behind him as he ran. There were none in front, but the animal scent was enough to tell him the Taz demon hadn't disappeared.

As Will reached the bottom of the steps, he could see Taz at the top, pushing clear the stone up into the crypt. Even as Will started running up the stairs, Taz jumped up with a single leap into the room above. Will did the same when he got to the top, and looked around urgently, but saw no one.

He heard Eloise behind him, her pace slowing with fatigue as she reached the top of the steps. He turned and pulled her up, then stepped into the open as she said, "Where did he go?"

He was wondering the same thing because the animal scent hung in the air of the crypt.

Will walked over and checked the gate—it was locked,

though he hardly imagined that being a barrier to a demon that could shift its shape so easily. He turned to face Eloise again and caught her shocked expression a moment too late, just as a sudden and powerful blow struck his back. It was as if Taz had emerged from the black iron of the gate itself.

Will flew heavily across the crypt, narrowly missing Eloise who scrambled out of the way. He crashed heavily against the far wall, with such a thud that he expected the mortar to fall from between the stones.

He jumped to his feet quickly, but Taz was already striding towards him. Will was ready this time. He stepped forwards and grabbed Taz by the arm, swinging him around and hurling him against the wall at the far end of the crypt.

Taz crashed into it with an impact that seemed to shake the foundations, and as with the others, he appeared to lose his shape, reforming briefly into a taller, broader human form before gelling back into the scrawny bully they'd met by the river.

He spotted Will and once again started towards him, but Will didn't give him a chance. He ran at full speed and slammed himself into Taz's body, knocking him backwards. There was another explosive crash as they hit the wall. Once again, Taz's face altered visibly, and the face it became was somehow familiar to Will, but it had changed back before he could identify it.

Will guessed there was only one way to get a second

look, so he grabbed Taz by the collar and threw him across the crypt, on a direct course for the tomb of Will's half-brother. But just as Will expected to hear a deafening crash, Taz's body passed through the stone and vanished.

Will stared in disbelief as Eloise said, "Did you see that? He went right through the stone, like it wasn't even there."

Will suddenly heard his name called out, a child's voice, yet eerie, a voice full of fear as if crying for help. "Will!"

Will and Eloise looked at each other and both stepped towards his brother's tomb, because it was from there that the cry had emerged.

"Will!" The cry came again as if somewhere that child searched for him.

As they reached the tomb, Taz emerged from the top of it and stood looking at them. He was still half sub-merged and was visible only from the waist up. He looked like he was standing in a stone-gray pool.

Taz didn't try to attack this time, but gazed around the crypt and at Will in some degree of confusion. It was as if this was no longer a demon at all, but the boy himself, transported into the confusing dream of his life.

But then, like that dog with pepper on its nose, Taz shook his head violently and there standing in front of Will was the face he'd seen in only the briefest snatches as he'd slammed the demon against wall after wall.

And yet, if Will wasn't mistaken, the face still wasn't completely fixed. As it stared at him, it seemed to be changing constantly, not in likeness but in age. And as it fleetingly reached its own childhood before melting into its older self, Will finally realized why it had looked so familiar and why this tomb had proved no barrier to it.

"Edward," said Will, his shock arising out of the immediate familiarity of that child's face even after seven and a half centuries. Edward, a fellow left-hander, taught to fight by Will, with Will's strengths and also his weaknesses—he understood everything about the demons now, even if he couldn't quite understand why Edward had sent them.

Whatever the reason, it hardly mattered at the moment, so overcome was he by the potent mix of emotions he felt at seeing Edward again. The tension and the anger rippling beneath his brother's face counted for little when set against the comfort that face provided, a glimpse back into the living world of his childhood, one that he thought he'd lost forever.

He turned and said to Eloise, "It's my brother."

By the time he turned back, it was the sterner older man who faced him, the man his brother had become, and even though the face occasionally lurched back to versions of its younger self, this was the dominant side of him, and the side that spoke now, snapping Will back into the present.

"So you recognize me, Will—I am pleased." A yelp emerged from the tomb and suddenly a small wire-haired terrier leapt through the stone lid and into Edward's arms. Edward looked down at it dotingly as he stroked its head. "There you are, boy." Then he said to Will, "He was buried with me, and our pagan ancestors were right—they do keep us company in the afterlife. I'm only sorry they didn't bury my horse with me—"

Will interrupted him and said, "What do you want, Edward? Why have you been attacking me? Why do you want my death?" Despite all the efforts he'd made, Edward now seemed uninterested in addressing his brother, but fussed instead over his dog, which he held in his arms like a baby. Will decided to draw him out and said, "By the way, I recognize your appearance. I recognize you as my late half-brother, but don't think I will ever recognize your title."

"You died!" The angry response was instant, Edward's voice thundering with such rage that the small dog leapt once more from his arms and disappeared back through the stone as easily as it would once have dived into the river. "You died the night we burned the witches. Accept that fact! You were *never* the Earl of Mercia. You died."

"If I am dead, what business have you with me now?"

At first, Edward could find no answer, but then his face grew threatening and he said, "I have no choice in this. It is a dark business that keeps you walking and now you seek to make it darker. You have become a devil and your destiny is a path of destruction." His tone softened a little. "I know not what remains of the brother I worshipped, but if there is anything of Will left within you, I implore you to stop."

Will shook his head, saying, "Edward, I am still entirely the brother you knew. I cannot stop, whatever my destiny proves to be, because for seven centuries and more, while you have been at peace, this body has been my prison, and I must find out why."

"So be it," said the ghost. "If you will not stop of your own accord, I will stop you and will not rest until the death is yours that you've so long refused to accept. The honor of our family demands it!"

"You think this fate has been of my choosing?" Edward did not answer. "And do you not think the honor of our family has been uppermost in my thoughts across all these centuries?"

Edward found his voice again, tinged with sadness, perhaps even shame, as he said, "Then tell me, Will, what honor do you bring to our family now, a parasite, surviving by bringing death to the people it was once your duty to protect? What honor is there in that?"

"None," said Will, feeling wounded, his heart pierced by the thought that his own brother could look upon him with such contempt.

He stumbled backwards, as if he'd lost his balance, and then he heard Eloise, her voice cracking slightly as she said, "Why now?" He looked at her and she cleared her throat and said, "You've been undead for seven centuries—ask him why he's waited till now."

Will turned and met Edward's stern gaze. "Why *have* you waited all this time, Edward?"

Edward's composure flickered, but he collected himself quickly and said, "What is time to the dead?"

"But why now?" Will stepped forwards, keeping his eyes fixed on his brother. "I have been a prisoner for hundreds of years, and it is true, I've brought little honor to our family in that time, but now it seems I might finally find the truth of what happened to me, perhaps avenge the act itself and regain the very honor you speak of. So why? Why would you choose to destroy me now? I am your brother, Edward—why would you deny me this opportunity of redeeming myself in your eyes?"

"I don't know, I . . ."

"You must!"

"You don't understand . . ." Edward cocked his head to one side, almost as if he could hear someone speaking far away. "I had to come."

Will was insistent. "But why, Edward?"

"I don't . . ."

Edward began to look flustered and confused, and as he did so, the years swept from his face, leaving him younger and younger, until finally he was once again the child Will had known.

The young Edward looked around as if he could see things that were not there, and then stared helplessly at his brother and said, "I'm afraid, Will. I'm afraid."

"Why did you come, Edward? I can't protect you if you

don't tell me." And even as Will said the words, he felt guilty because he could offer his brother no protection at all.

Perhaps Edward saw the lie in it, too, because he immediately transformed back into his older self and said sadly, "How can you protect me? You're only a boy."

"It's true, I'm only a boy, so I ask you again, why do you seek to destroy me?"

The flicker of uncertainty vanished and Edward looked fierce as he said, "Because you are a thing of darkness. You look and talk and move like my brother only because you have imprisoned his soul."

"That's a lie."

"Then come with me now." Edward paused after issuing the challenge, then added, "If you are my brother, what do you have to fear in death? It's where you belong, with your family, with the world you knew. If you were my brother, you would relish the opportunity of such a reunion."

Will felt himself drawn to the comforting warmth of that past, but even as his thoughts raced away into the sunlit morning of his childhood, he heard himself say, "I can't. I have unfinished business here."

"Exactly, because you are *not* my brother, not anymore. You are a thing possessed and I will not cease until I bring you death and give my true brother the peace he deserves."

Eloise whispered insistently, "He still hasn't said why he came now. You have to push him."

Will ignored her and said, "You want me to come with you now?"

"That is all I ask," said his brother.

"Will, you can't!"

"How about we arm-wrestle for it?"

Edward looked a little confused by the suggestion, but Eloise was outraged, saying, "You've *got* to be kidding!"

"How about it, Edward? You win, I come with you. I win, you leave me alone."

"Will, please don't do this. It's crazy!"

He turned and smiled at her, trying to offer some reassurance, even though he knew it probably did sound like madness to Eloise. By the time he turned back, Edward's elbow was resting on the surface of the tomb in readiness. Will leaned opposite and clasped his brother's hand.

They looked into each other's eyes and, without needing to say any more, they braced. Edward had the strength of the man he'd become, but had apparently brought little more than that from the spirit world. Will was easily stronger, but he exerted just enough pressure to push his brother's hand slowly towards the surface of the tomb.

"You remember this, Edward? You remember we did this as children?"

"Never mind that," said Eloise. "Just keep pushing."

"I remember," said Edward, who stared at his own hand as if unable to explain the imbalance of strength.

Edward's hand was only centimeters away from the

tomb but now Will gradually eased the pressure, allowing his brother to steal back a centimeter, then another. This was how easy it would be, he thought, to surrender himself to the grave. Talking to Edward had made him so homesick for that world.

Eloise was frantic, shouting, "Will, come on! You almost had him!"

He let her words fall unheeded, and now his hand was back past the halfway mark and Edward was straining hard. Will pushed back hard enough to make it difficult, but not enough to stop Edward's victorious momentum. And as Will's hand finally hit the hard surface of the tomb, he only hoped he'd judged his brother correctly.

"No!" shouted Eloise. She looked devastated and said, "But I've only just met you."

"It's fine," said Will. "Really, it's fine."

Edward had already let go of Will's hand and was staring at him in shock. Far from being triumphant, it was he who looked as if he'd seen a ghost, as if in the simple course of that contest, Will had demonstrated a truth and love that still held after seven centuries and more.

"You always did let me win," said Edward, moved by the memory of it. And as Will had hoped, it had been enough to bring Edward to the fore, the recollection of those childhood years when Will had been so much bigger than him and yet had always let Edward win.

"Yes, I did, brother, but this I ask: it is your turn to let me win."

"I can't," said Edward automatically.

"Do you not accept that I am fully your brother?"

"How could I ever have doubted it?"

"Then let me go."

"I can't," he said again, though in his eyes he appeared to be fighting it.

"Why?"

"I can't. He . . ." Edward stopped abruptly, as if his mind had run into a solid obstacle. He reached out and clasped Will's hand in both of his and closed his eyes, a look of intense concentration gripping his face, as if he was trying to overpower some hypnotic trance into which he'd been placed, and when he spoke again, he had to fight to get the words out. "I . . . was . . . summoned. He . . . has me in . . . his power."

"Who?"

It was almost painful to watch him struggle so, but at last, he seemed to break through the barrier and said clear and strong, "Wyndham!"

Wyndham—at the mention of this name the very stones of the crypt rumbled and moaned around them. There were other noises, too, far off, the sound of horses galloping, of wails and cries, anguish, the clatter of battle. And laughter.

But the laughter was Edward's, apparently happy that he'd finally defied the person who had raised him from the underworld, the person whose bidding he'd been doing until now.

"Who is Wyndham?"

A hand leapt out of the stone and started to pull at Edward's arm. He let go of Will and prized it off casually, still smiling, victorious as he said, "A sorcerer, Will." The walls and floor of the crypt were vibrating now, and the disturbed noises coming from the depths were loud enough that Edward had to raise his voice to be heard. He was struggling physically, too, as more tortured hands clawed at him, trying to pull him back into the tomb. He fended them off as he said, "He's a sorcerer, and he will not stop until he destroys you, but he will not use me again, I swear to it."

He was being pulled down, back into the tomb, and was already submerged to the chest.

Urgently, Will asked, "This Wyndham, is he also known as Lorcan Labraid?"

Edward laughed, even as the hands clawed at his face. "Lorcan Labraid! Will, you must know that Wyndham is dangerous, and powerful, too, powerful enough to summon me from beyond, to hypnotize me with thoughts of destroying you. You forgive me, Will, don't you?"

"Of course, Edward."

Edward nodded, even as he was pulled lower. "Wyndham is dangerous, but even *he* fears Lorcan Labraid—there is no greater evil in the world, and be warned, Will, your destiny will lead you there."

Will tried to ask another question, but it was already too late—Edward had been pulled back beneath the surface of the tomb. The rumbling of the stones stopped, so, too, the cries of the underworld. A few seconds later, a whistle sounded in the distance far below them, the whistle of someone calling to a dog. Sure enough, a small dog responded, its bark growing steadily fainter as it returned to its master.

Edward was gone. The stillness of the crypt settled once more about them, its peace restored, for the rest of the family at least. Will stared at the cold marble of the tomb, a troubled mix of happiness and sorrow sweeping over him.

"He really was a beautiful child, you know. I think I've missed him more than I knew."

Eloise's scent grew stronger, and he felt her hand rest upon his arm, the life force in her filling him instantly with a strange mixture of hunger and longing. He turned to face her and she smiled, offering comfort, but he could see that she was worried.

"Who's Wyndham?"

Will shook his head as he leaned against the tomb, and said, "A sorcerer apparently. One who's willing to summon up spirits, even my own brother, to destroy me."

He suddenly felt desperately lonely and homesick, not for this place that he still inhabited, but for the time that was his, for the family, for whatever spirit world Edward had returned to with his faithful dog.

"And Lorcan Labraid?"

"Someone Jex mentioned—he said Lorcan Labraid

is calling to me. And that he's the evil of the world."

"Nice. And I'm guessing this is all new to you?"

"Yes. As I told you, for more than seven hundred years there has been nothing. And now sorcerers are trying to destroy me, my own victims give me messages from the grave, the evil Lorcan Labraid calls to me."

"Do you think . . ." Eloise hesitated before saying, "Do you think Lorcan Labraid might be the one who bit you?"

"Possibly. I don't know." But the thought of that creature, whether Labraid or some other, was enough to bring Will back to the present. He couldn't know why Wyndham wanted to destroy him, nor why Lorcan Labraid called to him, but he could at least avenge the act that had started this and regain the family honor that had meant so much to Edward, and to him. "The notebook must hold the key, and if there's one thing I can do, it's to confront that creature at last."

"Now we're talking," said Eloise. She hesitated then and said, "But er, I need to pee first. Do you have a toilet down there?"

"No. I think there are some in the church."

"But what do you do?" Her thoughts immediately provided her with the only possible answer. "Don't tell me, you don't . . . go to the toilet . . . at all?"

"Do you really find that stranger than the fact that I have no discernible heartbeat, that my strength is out of proportion to my size, that I neither eat nor drink, that with the exception of my hair and teeth and nails, my body remains unchanged from one century to the next?"

"I suppose when you put it like that." She started towards the crypt gate, but stopped and smiled, saying, "You met me for a reason, Will. We're going to find him, and we're going to find out why this happened to you."

He nodded and smiled back. He wanted to believe her, but more importantly, he believed *in* her because she knew already that he was quite lost, more lost than she would ever be, and yet she still believed in him.

14

Will looked along the darkened nave as he waited for Eloise. It was no longer quite the same place it had been earlier, before that first attack. He no longer expected another demon, or at least he knew in his heart that Edward would trouble him no further.

But the air was charged now, as if the gates of the underworld were slowly opening, as if a great storm was about to break, and after all those centuries of emptiness, here he was at the center of it.

"Will?" He looked towards the cathedral toilets. Eloise sounded a little nervous as she said, "Could you come in here, please?"

He ran to the door and pushed it open, and even though she'd been careful to turn on only one light, he was momentarily blinded. As his eyes adjusted he saw her standing in the middle of the room, quite safe, but staring uneasily at the mirrors above the washbasins.

"What is it?"

"Look in the mirrors—tell me what you see."

He didn't understand. "I've told you, I cast a reflection."

"No, I mean, look *in* the mirrors."

Out of the corner of his eye then he spotted something moving in the mirrors. He looked across the room, but there was nothing there. He drew closer and immediately saw that there were shadowy figures beyond the glass, as if they were windows looking on to some dulled room, just visible beyond the reflection of tiled walls.

They were hooded, wearing dark robes, so at first Will thought they were monks, but almost immediately he realized from their silhouettes that they were women. He tried to see their faces but couldn't and every time one came close she seemed to keep her face hidden from him.

"They're whispering," he said because he could hear it now.

"I thought they were. Can you hear what they're saying?"

"No," he said, lying, not wanting to tell her what it was. "I can't see their faces either."

"I saw them," she said, her voice sounding small. He turned to look at her and she said, "They don't have any. They're just blank, or almost blank."

Will looked into the mirrors again, but the women all seemed to be walking away from them now. A moment later, they were gone and the reflection showed only the bright room in which they stood.

Eloise smiled and said, "I suppose they were ghosts. I expect you've seen plenty of ghosts in here over the centuries."

"Not until now." That response seemed to trouble her, so he added, "Still, at least they meant us no harm."

She seemed lost for a response, but then laughed and said, "Now *that* is a positive outlook. Shall we go?"

Will nodded and they walked back out into the nave, turning off the light as they left.

Eloise was mesmerized all over again by the misty half-light of the cathedral, so he slowed and eventually stopped for her to stand looking out at it.

"It's so beautiful—I'd never really noticed that before, not until I met you." She looked at him and said, "It was built before you were born, wasn't it?"

He nodded. "The main part of it was constructed long before, but it was still a work in progress—the Lady Chapel was being built when I was a child."

She laughed, as if she still couldn't quite believe that he was nearly as old as this building, then said, "Oh well, back to the crypt, I suppose." But they'd hardly taken a step when she stopped again and said, "The Heston-Dangraves crypt! That's your family name!"

"It was my family name in later years."

"I don't know why I didn't think of it before—I go to Marland Abbey School, or at least I did. They've probably expelled me. But that can't just be coincidence, can it, that my school is where your family moved after the dissolution?"

He smiled, being reminded of his family's history like that. Henry VIII had destroyed Marland and his brother's descendants had been given the lands. They'd built the sprawling Jacobean mansion that was now the school Eloise spoke of, and in the nineteenth century they'd built a Gothic mansion next to the ruins of the abbey itself. But even that mansion was no longer a home, owned instead by the National Trust.

The titles had died out long ago, and the last of the family—two elderly sisters who'd never married—had passed away fifty years ago. It made him sad to think of the family's achievements, of the undoubtedly fine houses they'd built—though he had never seen them for himself—and all of it gone.

His entire family, all those Mercian Earls and the Heston-Dangraves who'd followed them, was lost in time, the noble line crumbling to dust in the graves of two childless sisters. He was the only one left, and he was not enough.

"What's wrong? You look sad."

"It's nothing, just that I knew Marland well as a boy. We were there in the weeks before my sickness. I haven't seen it since of course, and nor would I recognize it if I did." He sighed. "It all seems such a very long time ago."

Eloise stepped closer, her voice almost a whisper as she said, "Will, when was the last time someone gave you a hug?"

He tried to think of an answer, even though the answer was obvious and it was merely the question that had thrown him, but before he could reply, Eloise put her arms around his waist and held herself against him in a brief embrace, nestling her head on his shoulder.

He was conscious of his hands hanging limply, but wasn't sure what he should do with them. He made to speak again, but as he did so, she pulled away slightly and kissed him. Her lips were soft and then he felt the tip of her tongue against his, the briefest moment of intense pleasure, but at that instant, the taste became overwhelming.

He could taste her blood. Her lips, her tongue, every corpuscle, the metallic richness of it pumping through every vein, through her beating heart. And even though he knew his teeth were filed, the animal instinct aroused by the taste of her made him want to bite into her lips, to draw that blood to the surface.

He'd seen her beauty from the start, had felt a strong enough connection with her that he'd been foolish enough to imagine such an intimacy as this. But this was the reality of it, the barren, hateful reality of his loneliness.

He pushed her away, too firmly, so much so that she looked shocked and upset.

"I'm sorry," he said. He tried to say more, but a violent pain tore through his head, cleaving his brain in two. He bent double, holding his skull tight, feeling if he didn't, it would blow apart.

"Will, what's wrong? Are you okay?" She sounded worried now, but also a little scared.

"Yes. I'm sorry. You don't understand." He couldn't say any more, until slowly the pain subsided, and the memory of that taste faded. Finally, he stood straight and looked at her, and felt wounded again for her hurt expression.

"Eloise, please don't think I'm blind to your beauty." He remembered the vision he'd had of her, of the two of them walking on that summer afternoon, and he wished so much that such an afternoon could be real, that they could have both lived those other lives. He smiled at the thought and said, "If you had been alive seven hundred and fifty years ago, I would gladly have broken my heart over you, but you weren't, and I'm not made for love, not the way I am now. When you kissed me, I could taste only blood. Your blood. Don't you understand? It's too much for me to bear."

"You mean, I taste like dinner." He laughed a little in response. She laughed, too, but then grew serious again and said, "Actually, what's really weird is that you don't taste of anything. You taste of nothing at all."

"I am nothing," he said simply.

"I don't believe that," she said, shaking her head. Then she shrugged. "Well, as we're not going to be making out for the rest of the night, we might as well get down to work on deciphering that notebook."

Will smiled. He didn't know what "making out" was, but he was relieved because she was joking and light-hearted, after everything that had happened. Eloise knew how little reason there was to be with him, she knew that he'd become something less than human, but she didn't run.

She wanted to help him find the one who'd bitten him, even if it was Lorcan Labraid, the evil of the world, who was apparently so much a part of Will's destiny. And it seemed she wouldn't be frightened off, not by demons or the ghost of his brother or the strange spirits they'd seen in the mirrors.

Yet the memory of those spirits troubled Will. He remembered what they had whispered and he tried to answer the question in his own mind, determined as he was that he would not lose her. And still that whispered question echoed in his thoughts, all the more disturbing because he had heard it before: "Will you sacrifice her, when the time comes?"

15

People can go entire lifetimes and fail to learn important things about themselves. So do not judge me too harshly when I say that I was five hundred years old before I fully understood that my only long-term relationship would be with loss—it has been the one certainty of my life, that I will lose everyone sooner or later.

By the late seventeenth century, merchants had become the dominant force in the city and they displayed their wealth by building large houses in the countryside immediately to the north of the city walls. At first this upset me greatly because the fields and woodlands there had been a favorite haunt of mine in the short summer nights. But progress can never be halted, and I continued to walk beyond the North Gate even as the landscape became swallowed up and transformed into an elegant extension of the city.

Indeed, the new houses and their inhabitants exerted a grim fascination over me, even after the countryside that I'd loved had been lost for several decades. So it was that I met Arabella.

Hers was a fine house set in walled gardens—the house is still there, though not as grand as it once was, and most of the gardens have long since been eaten up by other buildings.

One summer night in 1714 I was passing by on my way back into the city when I caught the unmistakable scent of blood in the gardens beyond the walls. Even at this time, people ventured out little at night, for fear of brigands and spirits, and though it was warm, the sky was moonless and dark.

I vaulted on to the wall and looked down upon the gardens to see just such a spirit traversing the lawns and walking among the flower beds. Dressed in white flowing nightclothes, her long hair a flourish of golden waves, her skin milk pale, she appeared like a ghost or an angel, floating through the darkness.

This was the then thirteen-year-old Arabella, and I was immediately smitten by her beauty. I descended into the garden and approached carefully through the shadows. And only after following her for some time did I come to understand that she was sleepwalking.

That first night, I was as mesmerized by her as my victims have been mesmerized by me. She walked for an hour before suddenly looking up into the night sky, and then she returned to the house just as if she had been called.

I looked at the sky myself and realized that I'd observed her too long, so bewitched had I been. I ran back into the city, reaching the crypt only as my skin began to prickle in discomfort at the approaching dawn, but I laughed and smiled the whole way, exhilarated.

I had seen her only once, but nothing had moved me so much in nearly five hundred years. If I had been a boy like any other, I would have declared myself in love.

I returned every night for the next week, and at first there were nights when I waited, but she did not come. Soon I realized that the sleepwalking only occurred on the warmest and most sultry evenings.

I chose the nights of my visits accordingly and so learned to read the weather and her nocturnal state well enough that I was rarely disappointed.

One night the following summer, the moon was full, but I was still there in her garden despite the burning discomfort of its reflected light on my skin. Even when I kept to the shadows, the prickling sensation of heat flared across my flesh. Yet little did I care because the night was warm and Arabella walked abroad. It was a distraction like none I'd known.

She had been walking only for a few minutes and was moving away from me across a lawn when she stopped and turned to face me.

I assumed she was still in the deeps of sleep, but with a curious tone, she suddenly said, "Hello." Perhaps I should not have responded, but I did, and then she said, "Step out from the shadows that I might see you."

I moved forwards, shielding my eyes as well as I could against the moonlight, and said, "I mean you no harm."

She was about to reply sternly, but studied me in the faint blue light of the moon and said, "I know your face, as if I've seen you before. Who are you?"

"I'm William . . ." I stopped myself in time, remembering that any reference to my birth would arouse her suspicions. "Please, call me Will."

She adopted a haughty air, something she managed even in her nightclothes, and said, "And you may call me Miss Harriman."

I almost laughed, not least at the thought of a merchant's daughter taking such airs with me, but I accepted her invitation graciously and said, "Thank you, Miss Harriman. But might I at least know your name?"

"Arabella." Without my asking, she volunteered, "I'm fourteen."

"I'm four hundred and seventy-five."

She looked me up and down and said, "Then you are a Will-o'-the-wisp, though dressed in the latest fashion, and I must go to my bed in fear of my soul." She laughed playfully and walked away across the lawn, saying, "Good night, Will-o'-the-wisp."

"Good night, Miss Harriman," said I.

At that time, no girl of her age could have been expected to behave as Arabella had done. If she'd believed me flesh and blood, she should have run in terror, fearing for her honor and her life. If she'd believed me a sprite, she should have screamed in terror for her soul.

Yet no matter what the conventions of the age, some people find their own path and she was one such. On the nights that she woke from her walking slumber, she would converse with me, sometimes for only a few minutes, sometimes for as much as an hour.

I never sought to wake her, and her night walks were confined to the warmest months, but over the next few years we spoke several dozen times, always in an elliptical fashion, as if she didn't believe me

quite real, but rather an imaginary friend who came
to her in her dreams.

Perhaps it seems a great commitment on my part,
to find my way to that same garden so many times
over several years, but set against the span of my life
thus far, I look back upon it now as you might upon
a fleeting summer romance.

There was no romance, though the brief moments
in her company warmed and restored me. I knew
enough to know that I would have loved her if I had
been able, if part of my curse had not been the loss
of that physical emotion.

And the real curse was that I had not lost the
memory of love, not lost my longing for things I'd
once known. So in the year that Arabella was seventeen, I waited in vain through the warm nights like
any lovesick youth would have done, but she never
appeared again.

I wondered if she'd been struck down by some ill-
ness or other in the previous months, or if she had
been married off and sent away. For several years I
drifted around the city in the hope of seeing her,
drawing as close to the lit world of affluent houses
as I dared.

And it was not until the winter of 1742, long after
hope had gone, that I saw her again. There was some
entertainment in the city's recently constructed hall,
drawing the coaches of society families from all around.

I was observing from the shadows, as I've observed so much of the history and life of this city, and then I saw her. Arabella descended from a coach, and apart from the evening clothes she wore, she had changed little more than I had in the intervening years.

I was so transfixed to see her again, and so unexpectedly, that I took several paces towards her, my mind spinning with thoughts, clinging to the impossible hope that she had somehow become like me.

I was only a few meters away when the woman who accompanied her turned and fixed me with a stare, at first hostile, then puzzled. This woman was clearly the younger girl's mother, a woman of forty-two, much older then than it is now.

It was as her puzzled expression briefly appeared troubled by some distant recollection, as if she was remembering a recurring dream from her childhood, that I realized my mistake. For it was the older woman who was Arabella and as the recollection finally knitted itself together in her mind, I doubt she could have looked more horrified if death himself had confronted her.

I think she fainted, though I couldn't be sure. I heard the commotion only as I fled from the scene. And as I thought back to the way age had played itself out upon her face, I think I felt more alone than I have done at any other time over these seven and a half centuries.

That is why I tried to destroy myself because I realized at that moment that my life was nothing but a cruel trick played on me by fate. Just as the gods of Ancient Greece devised cruel and eternal punishments for those who had offended them, so I had been forced to live a half-life for eternity, with a withered heart and no hope of escape.

At least, almost no hope. Several years earlier, I had acquired a rare and unusual book—and, for all its faults, I still have it in my collection—which included the first account I'd ever read of creatures that shared most of the traits of my sickness.

Using the information gleaned from that book, I returned to my lair on the night I saw Arabella again, I fashioned a wooden stake, lay on my daybed, and plunged it with all my might into my heart.

The result was instantaneous, my strength falling away from me. I was immediately so physically weakened that my hands fell to my sides and I could no longer lift them. For the briefest moment, I was happy, sensing that death was upon me.

But death did not come. I screamed, not in pain, but in the agony of frustration, but I couldn't move myself. I was doubly imprisoned, firstly by my sickness and then by the stake I'd driven through my own heart.

It's impossible to describe the time I spent in that purgatory, pinned and helpless, yet fully conscious of my condition, hour after hour, day after day, year after year. I had thought that my condition could be no worse than it already was, but I was wrong.

The sleep of hibernation finally overtook me. When I awoke, the stake was gone from my heart and the wound had already greatly healed. I wish I could say that I felt joy, but I felt only as a criminal must when he is released from prison, but sent into exile.

I found the stake on the floor nearby. The wood had started to crack and I could only assume that this had reduced its hold on me, that I had somehow managed to tear it free in my sleeping state, just as the sleepwalking Arabella might once have removed a thorn from her hand or foot.

And yes, even freshly delivered from those decades of torment, I still thought of Arabella in the first days after my recovery. But a new world awaited me in the city above. Arabella was dead, so was the daughter with whom I had last seen her and everyone else arriving for that distant night's entertainment.

The year was 1813 and, though it had taken the best part of a century, I had learned a valuable lesson, that death wanted me no more than life did. I was forever suspended between those two states and I believed it would always be so.

She smiled and he felt exposed, wondering if she'd seen through his lie. But her mind skipped on and she tapped Jex's notebook where it lay on the bed next to her, saying, "Wasn't as difficult as I thought—all the prophecies are in block capitals. The rest is just like a diary or a journal."

"That was the impression I got."

"So!" She looked at her own notebook as she said, "Okay, there's nothing about Lorcan Labraid in here, nothing about Wyndham or the ghosts in the mirrors. But there's a guy called Asmund who gets a couple of mentions. First it says he waits with the sprites."

"Spirits."

"No, I thought it said that at first, but it's definitely sprites. Then it says, 'The church will speak, that lost its people, and Asmund is its voice.' And then, 'His maker awaits in the church that lost people and steeple.' His maker—that has to be a reference to the person who bit you, don't you think? Asmund's a vampire, and he's waiting in a church somewhere, for you, I guess." She stopped and shuddered slightly, as if hit by a chill, and said, "Didn't you see all of this when you looked through the book?"

"There was so much to take in," Will said, distracted though, because he sensed some shift in the atmosphere of the room, something troubling. Was that why she'd shuddered, because she sensed it, too?

Eloise looked at her notes again as she said, "Who

knew? Jex's notebook is guiding you to the one person you've been wanting to meet all this time."

And now Will knew what was wrong. Her breath rose up from her lips and hung in the air like mist as she absentmindedly reached for her coat and put it on. The temperature had dropped sharply as she'd unlocked this mystery for him, as if some unnatural presence had come into the room with them, drawn by her words.

So maybe she was right about the book leading him to the creature's hiding place. The creature had a name—Asmund—and if Will found Asmund, he would find out why this had been done to him, why he'd been chosen and not another, why he'd been denied his rightful place in history. Above all, he would have the chance to repay Asmund for the curse of this sickness.

Eloise was shivering slightly now, though she hardly seemed to notice it, even as she pulled her coat tightly around her. And as distorted as the atmosphere was becoming around them, as much as the temperature dropped, as much as this simple conversation seemed to unsettle the underworld, Will wanted to keep going. Worse, as much as he feared this could be dangerous for both of them, he couldn't stop himself.

"Then Asmund must serve Lorcan Labraid, and in that one person I'll have the key to my destiny, and more importantly, vengeance for what he did to me and my family."

She nodded, as if for the first time she truly understood

his cursed existence, and said, "So we have to find that church."

Even as she spoke, Will felt something behind him—not a scent, but a presence, almost as if someone had touched him on the shoulder. It unnerved him enough that he started to turn, but he was still facing Eloise when he heard a harsh, urgent whisper close to his ear.

"The time comes!"

He spun around, seeing only the empty chamber, the candles, the openings into the other chambers. But he could hear more whispering now, and he recognized the voices of the spirits they'd seen earlier.

Behind him, Eloise said, "You can hear it, too, can't you? Like whispering, like the women in the mirrors?"

He turned back to her and she looked small and frozen huddled there on the daybed, her skin almost blue with the cold. He nodded and she nodded back at him and said, "Good, it's not just me. And you probably haven't noticed, but it's turned really cold in here."

He stood and said, "The whispering, it's coming from in there." He pointed to the passageway into the rocky chamber with the pool in it.

She stood, too, making clear she was going wherever he went. He could hardly blame her. Will was unnerved himself because even Edward's spirit had struggled to enter these chambers uninvited, and because these spirits had briefly brought him back to his senses.

They seemed more concerned with Eloise than they

did with him and the thought of her being in danger now made him as fearful as it should have done a few minutes before. This was not her battle.

He walked into the passage, the whispers becoming louder. The voices weren't speaking in unison, but layered over each other, so that only the occasional word was audible. Even Will could probably only hear what they were saying because he had heard the phrase earlier.

"When the time comes . . . Will you . . . When the time comes . . . Will you sacrifice her, when the time comes?"

The question was so insistent that he began to doubt himself. He had no idea what he was leading Eloise into or if he'd be able to protect her. In the heat of the moment, might he be tempted? One more human life in exchange for . . . ? But he didn't want to think about it, not least because he knew in his soul that she was not just one more life.

The chamber was empty, but the whispering seemed all around them now, echoing off the rocky walls of the underground cave it had once been, sometimes sounding so close that Will kept turning, expecting to see one of the spirits behind him.

Eloise walked over to the pool and placed her candle at the side of it. She stared for a moment at the surface of the water, then said, "Er, you might want to look at this."

He stepped closer and looked down. Where the candle illuminated the water it had transformed, so that now it appeared as if they were looking down through a rippling, green-tinged window at a room far below. It was almost like the cloister of a convent and down there below walked the women in robes, whispering their constant prayer.

As with the mirrors in the church above, the moment Will looked down at the women, they seemed to sense his presence and slowly dispersed, walking beyond the edges of the vision till only the stone floor of the phantom cloister remained.

The water began to darken; the whispers grew more distant, but once again, Will got the unpleasant sensation of someone standing behind him. He turned and this time saw one of the robed figures, life-size and solid, disappearing into the passageway.

He followed, even though a part of him didn't want to, and Eloise hurried to pick up the candle and go after him. He caught another glimpse of the spirit ahead as it turned into the more structured passageway to his burial chamber. Even though he knew it had to be a spirit, the woman looked solid.

She'd gone from the passage by the time he stepped into it, but he knew there was only one place she could go. He stepped through into the burial chamber, Eloise immediately behind him, their candles illuminating the walls, the earth around the lip of the casket, the hooded figure standing with its back to them in the far corner.

The spirit didn't move, but stood facing the wall in silence.

"What do you want of me?" There was no response, and Will took a step forwards, but Eloise put her hand on his shoulder to stop him.

Eloise looked at the figure and repeated Will's question, "What do you want of me?"

This time there was a flicker of movement, as if the spirit responded in some way to her voice, and Eloise started to walk forwards herself. Even as Will admired her bravery, he was full of misgivings, not wanting the spirit to turn, not wanting to see the ghost of a face that Eloise had seen in the mirrors. Nor could he understand what it was that he dreaded so much about this spirit and its purpose here.

He sensed that Eloise wasn't in danger from the spirit itself, far from it, and yet he couldn't stop himself saying, "Eloise, wait."

Her hand was poised, ready to reach out and touch the woman, but she hesitated and then backed away as the robe started to crackle with energy, sparks flying off the fibers like so much static electricity. The figure appeared to be merging with the wall, the sparks forming together in ragged lightning patterns across the surface of the robe, becoming more intense.

The light became so bright that Will had to shield his eyes and when he lowered his hand again, only Eloise was standing there, the last remnants of the crackling lights dying out on the wall of the chamber.

"What happened?"

Eloise was still staring into the corner, transfixed, as she said, "She walked right through the wall." Still she stared for a moment or two, as if hoping the spirit would return, but finally she turned and said, "I'm not imagining it, am I? That spirit, she . . . she responded to me more than she did to you."

Will nodded and said, "For whatever reason, I think they're trying to protect you, and reminding me of what I should have known from the start, that this is my search and that I should do it alone."

Her face changed instantly, a glimpse of the unfriendly girl he'd first encountered by the river, and she sounded determined as she said, "No, I don't think it's that at all! You need me. I know you haven't needed anyone else for hundreds of years, but I think you need me. And you have to admit, even by your standards, there's some really strange stuff happening to you right now."

He felt like telling her that he had always needed someone, that the need had never gone away, but instead, he said, "Eloise, everything about my existence is strange. Is it not strange that I'm standing here talking to you seven hundred years after I should have died an old man? Perhaps you'll only fully understand how strange this is when you're seventy and I am still the boy you see before you now."

"That's if you're still alive." He looked at her questioningly and she said, "It just seems that from the minute you found that notebook, something was set in motion, that you'll find your destiny . . ." She waved her hand casually at the buried casket between them. "Or you'll die trying."

Will nodded a little in agreement. He still didn't want to tell her how appealing that last possibility sounded. Death was as tempting as a warm bed to a sleepy child, but before he surrendered, he had to know the truth. He had to know who had done this to him and why. If Asmund had been responsible, he wanted to know who he was and why he'd done it, whether for Lorcan Labraid or some other thing of evil and, of course, he wanted to repay him.

"Maybe I do need you to help me find Asmund, but . . ." He couldn't think of a way of ending the sentence without revealing what he'd heard the spirits saying, so he shrugged and said, "Let's go back into the other room."

Will stepped aside for her to go first, but stayed close behind her, even though the atmosphere had returned to normal and it was obvious that this visitation had ended.

Eloise walked back towards the daybed, but stopped short, pointing as she said, "Jex's notebook." It lay open on the daybed.

"What of it?"

She put the candle down and turned to Will as she said, "It wasn't open when I left it."

She was right. He remembered her tapping the closed book with her finger before she started reading from her own notes. She picked up the book now and looked at

158

the two open pages, trying to find what the spirit had so wanted them to see.

"The writing's hard to read—it's just one of his diary pages." She scanned it, then stopped and looked at Will, then back at the page, incredulous. "Why didn't I see this before?"

"What does it say?"

Chris and Rachel know the truth. They have seen and they know.

She pointed to the line in the middle of the dense script that filled both pages and Will nodded, even as he scanned the rest of what he could see, hoping that the spirits had been trying to leave some other message than this.

Eloise had already decided and said, "It makes sense—they knew Jex, so they'd be able to tell us about him. And maybe they can help us find the church."

Will shook his head.

"Impossible. Going to Chris and Rachel would mean telling them who I am or at least something of what I'm about—that's a risk I can't afford to take."

"Why not?"

"Because that's how I've survived all this time, by having as few people as possible know me." Eloise didn't seem convinced and he added, "Besides, I didn't tell you before, but something troubled me about their behavior, the way they stared at me, the way my wound flared up when they came near."

"Maybe for the same reason that the spirits opened

the book on this page, and why Jex wrote about them knowing, because they're part of this—they must have information we can use, and trust me, they're good people."

"Perhaps they are, but you also have to understand my need for caution. The spirits opened that book, but we don't know whether it was a sign or a warning. For all I know, those spirits are summoned by Wyndham, just as Edward's was."

"You know they weren't!" She sounded angry and certain, and hardly softened as she said, "Look, something led you to Jex, something led you to me, and now the same thing is leading you to Rachel and Chris. There's a good reason for it, I know there is, and I'm asking you to trust me on that."

Her determination to involve Chris and Rachel was surprising and, with a slight pang, a shadow of the rejection he'd known before, he wondered if she was already tiring of his cold company and wanting to be back with living people again.

"I do trust you, but I can't . . ."

"Then prove that you trust me!"

"You don't understand, I . . ."

"I heard them." Her voice was fierce and had a challenge in it, and in response to his look of confusion, she said, "I heard what the spirits said. Earlier, and again in the pool, about sacrificing me when the time comes?"

He was momentarily speechless, bewildered by the

revelation because she'd shown no signs of having heard
them. And he wondered if this was why she wanted to go
to Chris and Rachel—she'd been testing him and now she
feared that he *would* sacrifice her.

He said, "Why didn't you tell me?"

"Why didn't you?"

"Because I thought you might be frightened, that you
might want to leave, and I don't want you to leave. And
because whatever happens, I will never sacrifice you, no
matter what comes."

Eloise smiled a little and said, "That's what I hoped.
I've known you such a short time, but I already know
I can trust you completely. So now I'm asking you to
trust me."

Will shook his head in amazement, that she could have
so much faith in him after so short a time. He reached
out and took her hand in his, feeling the warmth and
the pulsing blood, wishing it did something more than
remind him of how much life she had to lose.

He looked down at her fingers covered in silver rings
and said, "Do you mind if I do something?" She shook her
head. "It's just that you have such beautiful hands. . . ."
He gently eased one ring free, then the other two, expos-
ing the pale, slender beauty of her fingers. He looked
down at her hand resting in his and was overcome with a
barrage of memories and half-memories, glimpses of the
life that might have been his.

Eloise looked down, too, and as if having the same

thoughts, she said, "Men are meant to put rings on a girl's finger, not take them off."

"If only I was a man like other men." Reluctantly, he let go of her hand and gave the rings back to her. "I'm afraid of what I might be leading you into, but I do trust you."

She smiled and said, "So we can go to see Chris and Rachel?"

He nodded and smiled, too. He'd already shown more trust in her than he had in anyone since the day of his sickness, and he knew he would yield to her on this, too. It was even possible that she was right about Chris and Rachel possessing knowledge he needed, but the thought of returning to the Whole Earth still filled him with unease because of all that he didn't know about them.

What had they seen? What did they know? Above all, if they meant him no harm, why had his ancient wound flared up in their company, reminding him that he had once been bitten, and of all the pain that had since flowed from it?

17

It was approaching eleven and the mood in the city was edgy and volatile. Groups of young men and women moved about the streets, many of them drunk, shouting and laughing. For now, the crowds were still light-hearted, but the promise of violence was everywhere.

Perhaps it was because of the strangeness of the last few days, but Will also sensed, as he had before, that the threatening air about the streets was being caused by something greater than the drink-fueled ugliness they could see all about them.

It was as if the city itself was preparing for some impending catastrophe. There had always been talk of ghosts and darkness here, even in his boyhood, and now that darkness seemed to be seeping from the stones and timbers as much as it was descending from the heavens.

What he didn't know was whether he saw this now only because of his own mood, because of the confusing events overtaking him, or whether the disturbance he felt all around him was real and, worse, if it was happening because of him.

He supposed he and Eloise made a dramatic pair—pale and dressed in black. Their appearance made them stand out from the crowd and Will heard a couple of snide remarks here and there, similar to the ones Taz had made, but they kept their heads down and walked on.

Eloise could hear the comments, too, and at one point she said, "It's funny, I hate violence, but it's nice knowing you could probably see off all these people if you wanted to."

"Yes, I could," he said. "Except my existence relies upon keeping a low profile. It's why I'm uneasy about meeting your friends again."

"But you're still coming," she said, pointing out the obvious.

"I'm still coming," he said, and smiled, and they turned into one of the narrower streets where it was quieter.

It was eleven by the time they got to the Whole Earth and the last customers were just leaving. Chris was saying good-bye to them and clearing tables, but his expression changed when he saw Will and Eloise approaching. He looked at them expectantly as they reached the door.

"We need your help," said Eloise.

Chris looked as if this was something he'd hardly dared hope for and said eagerly, "Of course, come in." He stood to one side and then locked the door behind them, changing the sign from OPEN to CLOSED.

He stood for a moment, indecisive, and then Rachel came out of the main room and smiled broadly as she saw them. "Hello, you two! This is a nice surprise."

"They need our help," said Chris. Will saw the same expression in Rachel's eyes, that of someone whose lucky day had come. He knew this was wrong, and not just because of the wound on his arm, which was almost burning in their presence. Just standing there with them, he felt like a rare moth lured into their light trap. Only Eloise's reassuring looks kept him from running back into the night.

Rachel smiled warmly and said, "Why don't you come with me through to the house?"

"I'll finish up out here," said Chris as Will and Eloise followed Rachel through the kitchen and into a connecting corridor.

The building had clearly been extended considerably at the back since its early days because Rachel now showed them into their sizeable, if rambling, living accommodation.

Bookshelves covered most of the walls, and where there weren't books there were crystals and odd little statues. It looked like a more cluttered version of the café.

Rachel showed them into a sitting room where two dark green sofas faced each other across an Oriental coffee table.

"Please, sit down. I was just about to have green tea— would you like some?"

"Thanks, I'd love some," said Eloise.

"Not for me, thank you."

"Can I get you something else?"

"Thank you, but I'm fine, really."

Rachel nodded before walking away.

Eloise took off her coat and sat on one of the sofas. Will remained standing for a moment until Eloise gestured for him to remove his own coat. He did so and sat next to her and looked casually at the walls of books, some of which looked old and rare enough that he might consider them for his own collection.

Eloise was looking around, too, and said, "Isn't this great? I really like the feel of the place."

Will nodded and said quietly, "Haven't you been here before?"

"Not in the house part."

He wondered if she had a single suspicious bone because she didn't seem to consider it at all strange that Chris and Rachel should suddenly be giving them such special treatment. Even after Will had voiced his concerns, Eloise still couldn't see anything sinister here, only good people and honest hospitality.

Before he could say any more, Rachel came back in with a tray. There were three large cups of green tea and a plate with some type of coarse-looking biscuit on it.

She was just setting the tray on the table when Chris also came into the room and the two of them sat on the sofa opposite. As Rachel handed out the tea, she said, "Will, I feel awful you sitting there with nothing. Are you sure there isn't . . ."

"Really, I'm fine, but thank you for offering."

Rachel shrugged in surrender and offered the plate to Eloise. She took a biscuit just as Chris said, "So you said you needed our help."

The biscuit stayed suspended halfway to Eloise's mouth as she answered. "Yeah, we need you to tell us what you knew about Jex."

Will studied the couple closely as she said this. They didn't look at each other, perhaps because it would have been too obvious, given that they were both facing the same direction. But their reactions were almost identical—both looked slightly surprised, suggesting they were expecting a different question.

Chris hesitated, as if wondering whether he could move the subject back to what he really wanted to talk about, but then gave a big sigh and said, "We don't know a great deal. He'd been doing a doctorate at the university, theology, I think, but he dropped out years ago, went traveling, then came back here. That was when we first met him, only because he came in here. He became quite a regular."

Rachel added, "Chris helped him out with some money, but he insisted on repaying it a couple of months later."

Eloise looked frustrated and said, "Did he ever talk about the city, you know, about its dark side or about its history?"

Chris said, "Sure, he often babbled on about things like that. But then so do we."

Eloise tried one last time. "So there was nothing else unusual about him?" She used the end of the question to finally take a bite of the biscuit.

They both shook their heads, but then Rachel said, "Oh, except for the blackouts."

"Yes," said Chris. "Of course, I didn't think about that."

"He had blackouts. Had one in the café once, and while he was out, he began speaking in Latin."

Will said, "What did he say?"

"I don't know—it was Latin."

"You don't speak Latin?"

Chris looked incredulous and said, "Do you?"

"I do, a little," offered Eloise.

Will avoided answering by waving his hand at the room as he said, "I just thought you both must be very educated."

"I suppose we are," said Rachel, "but sadly, neither of us are linguists."

As if a door had somehow been opened to other matters, Chris said casually, "What about you, Will, where are you from?"

Will could feel Eloise become tense, and Rachel was equally on edge, trying too hard to look casual now. Chris was a better actor, remaining fresh-faced and open, as though it had been the most innocent question in the world.

Will understood intuitively that the time had come to find out what they were about. They knew something about him and he had to find out what it was before this went any further.

"Where I'm from is less important than where I am. Why have you allowed me into your house?" Rachel and Chris looked at each other, unsure how to respond. Eloise still seemed uncomfortable, but with Will's tone now rather than Chris's question. "You know nothing whatsoever about me, yet on our second meeting, here I am sitting in your home. Why? I doubt you afford this level of hospitality to even your most regular customers, so why would you do it for a stranger? Why am I here?"

If they were innocent, if they really knew nothing about him and he'd misinterpreted their stares and Jex's words, this was the moment at which they'd take offense and ask him to leave. They didn't.

Rachel and Chris sat immobile, unable or unwilling to answer. Eloise shifted slightly in her seat—he had the feeling she'd have run out of there in embarrassment if given half a chance. It was the kind of awkward social situation she probably spent most of her time trying to avoid and she was undoubtedly wondering why Will had stepped over that mark, but he knew he was right.

Finally, Rachel sighed heavily and said, "Show him." Chris looked at her questioningly and she said, "Chris, it wouldn't be the first time we've made complete fools of ourselves. Besides, I'm not in any doubt."

"Nor am I."

She nodded. "Get the laptop—show him."

Chris got up and left the room and came back a moment later with something that, to Will, looked like a large slim book made out of silver. He opened it up, placed it on the table in front of him, and pressed some buttons.

Chris looked at Eloise then and said, "You know we're massively into the occult, the supernatural. I mean, we're not witches or anything, but we're passionate about it."

Before Eloise could acknowledge the point, Rachel added, "We're trying to establish a chair of parapsychology at the university."

"That's amazing," said Eloise, apparently genuinely impressed.

Chris continued, "Well, I suppose we were always interested, but what I'm about to show you is what first really got us going. On the surface, it doesn't look much, but it made us both believe that there was more to this world than you see on the surface."

Chris turned the laptop sideways so that they could all see its screen. He was about to press another button, but Rachel stopped him, saying, "Hold on, you've got to tell them the background first. You can't just show the film."

"Of course," said Chris. Will got the impression they'd shared this so often, and the story was so familiar to the two of them, that Chris forgot the need to explain anything. "We were students at the university here. That's how we met, in our first year."

Rachel smiled at Eloise and said, "Can you believe it? We've been together ever since."

"That's beautiful," said Eloise.

"So it's in our first year, a spring night in 1989," said Chris, and Will immediately became uncomfortable, realizing that the date coincided with his last period of activity. "I'd just got a camcorder, which was really cool, and we were out to see how it worked at night, just fooling around in the square next to the cathedral, filming each other, being stupid."

"But the important thing is, it's the early hours and a weekday, and there was no one else about, no one at all."

"That's right," agreed Chris. "It was just the two of us, so we were pretty freaked out when we looked at the film later and there's a third person in shot. Was it a ghost? We had no idea, but it was eerie, I know that much."

Rachel shook her head at the memory of it and said,

"I can still remember the hairs on my neck standing up when we first watched it."

"So that's the story. Here's the film." Chris turned the laptop a little more, making it easier for them to see, then leaned over and pressed the button. A freeze-frame image appeared and then the film stuttered into life.

18

The film was as Chris had explained, first one, then the other, wrapped up against the cold, laughing and dancing, pulling faces at the camera. They looked dramatically younger in the film, almost as young as Eloise did now.

Off-camera, the younger Chris, his voice slightly higher than it was now, said, "Let's see if we can get both of us in shot."

There was some maneuvering before Chris, holding the camera at arm's length, managed to capture some wobbly footage of the two of them standing together. Rachel turned to Chris and they kissed, and the image spun away then as the camera was pointed at the floor. A few moments later, Rachel said, "Getting cold now, let's go."

The camera moved into a different position, randomly shooting the side of the cathedral as the two of them discussed what to do next. It was only a few seconds before Chris realized that the camera was still running and turned it off, but for the duration of those seconds, he'd filmed a figure standing in front of the cathedral wall, staring intently in their direction.

Will could understand why they'd thought the figure might be a ghost, not only because they hadn't seen it at the time of filming, but because of the deathly white face, the unusually sad expression. It had been taken only days before his last hibernation.

And the odd thing was he remembered the occasion because it seemed only a week or so ago in his mind. In each period of activity, the time would come when he needed blood, but did not want it, the earth calling him back more strongly than the hunger to keep going. This had been such a time.

He remembered seeing them—two people looking not much older than him, kissing, wrapped up in each other— and that feeling had intensified. It was instinct that drove him to hibernate, not choice, but he would have chosen it at that moment anyway because he saw that blood had nothing to offer him but more of this, standing in the shadows, watching other people live.

It had affected him so strongly and yet, until seeing the film, he'd allowed it to slip from his memory's grasp. The real surprise to him now was that he hadn't even thought Rachel or Chris familiar—true, in his eyes, they had aged twenty years in what had seemed a matter of days, but he should have recognized them from that night.

Chris leaned forwards and turned the laptop towards him, fiddling with the buttons before turning it back. The screen was now frozen on the image of the figure standing in front of the cathedral wall.

"That's why you're in our house," said Chris. "It *is* you, isn't it, Will?"

Was this what Jex had meant in his journal, when he'd said that they had seen, that they knew?

"Yes, it's me."

They looked staggered, even though it would have been ridiculous to deny it. But their response made him wonder if they were ready for the truth they'd actually stumbled upon.

Chris said, "But this was taken twenty years ago."

"You look exactly the same," added Rachel. "How is that possible? You're not a ghost."

"He's a vampire." Chris, Rachel, and Will all looked at Eloise. She turned to Will and looked apologetic as she said, "Sorry. But how else could you explain it?"

Rachel tried to start a sentence several times and finally said, "When Ella said you're a vampire, what exactly . . . ?"

"Er, as we're being truthful and everything, my name's actually Eloise."

Chris looked at her in a way that suggested even this simple admission was a shock to him. "But you're not a vampire?"

Eloise laughed and said, "Of course not! You've seen the way I eat."

"I prefer the term undead," said Will, and all eyes were once again on him, no less than if he'd sought to mesmerize them. "I've been trapped inside this body since the night the witches burned in 1256, and since the winter of 1263, I have been, in the eyes of God if no one else, William, Earl of Mercia."

"Of course you have," said Rachel, clearly in a state of shock. "You're nearly eight hundred years old and here you are, sitting on our sofa, and you're a vampire who needs our help. Of course."

"I prefer the term undead," repeated Will.

"I don't get this," said Chris. "That's definitely you in the film, so as crazy as it seems, I have to go with the whole undead thing, but where have you been all this time? Where do you live? How? I mean, how did you become a vamp . . . undead?"

"I can't tell you where I live, and I'm searching even now for the one who bit me. That's why we're here—Eloise thinks you may be able to help us find him."

They stared at Will, taking in what he was saying, but still waiting for answers to their own questions. Of course they wanted answers; it was a natural desire, just as natural as his tendency to despair at the questions because, ultimately, he knew little more than they did.

A part of him wished he could hibernate right now, that he could disappear deep underground and resurface again in another lifetime, move things along at a pace that suited him. But that choice wasn't his, and whatever force controlled his existence, it had decided that now was the time for his reckoning.

"On the night the witches burned, I was sixteen years old, heir to the Earldom of Mercia. . . ."

Will told them his tale as briefly as possible and all three sat entranced as they listened, even Eloise who'd heard much of it before. He described the nature of his condition, or at least as much of it as he knew himself, and ended with a revelation that still seemed to shock Rachel and Chris, despite all that had come before it.

"I hibernated a few days after you captured my image, and awoke a few days ago. I needed blood and selected what I believed was a random victim, someone who would not be missed, your friend Jex. But I no longer believe I chose him at all, for in his possession I found a notebook." Will reached into the pocket of his overcoat and pulled out the book. "This notebook. It talks of me, and it mentions you, which is why we're here, even though, you'll understand, it's against my instincts to trust anyone."

"You can trust us," said Rachel, and looked so sincere that he wanted to believe her.

Chris shook his head, saying, "But how on earth do you expect us to help? Don't get me wrong, we're willing, I just can't see what we can do."

Eloise answered. "You can help us understand some of the prophecies in the book. There's a church we need to find, a place that might be the lair of Asmund—we think he's the vampire who bit Will."

"It might not even be close by," said Will. "The notebook talks of a church that lost people and steeple."

Rachel stared at Eloise questioningly and said, "How do you two know each other?"

"He rescued me."

"Possibly because I was meant to," added Will. Eloise looked at him, surprised by the comment, and he smiled a little and said, "In some way or other, I think Eloise might be part of my destiny. Perhaps you are, too."

Will didn't say in which way they might be part of it, for good or ill, but Chris nodded at the final comment, as if he felt that, too. He seemed to be over the shock now and sounded briskly efficient as he held his hand out and said, "Let me have the notebook. I'll run it through the copier and we'll find out what we can."

Will handed him the book, but said, "You'll give it back?"

"In a minute or two," said Chris as he took the book and left the room.

Rachel also emerged suddenly from her shocked state and said, "A church that lost its people—do you think it could be a lost village?"

"I've seen them on TV," said Eloise enthusiastically. "You can see the outlines from the air. They were wiped out in the plague or something."

The plague—it seemed his whole life had been set against the backdrop of one plague or another. But Will also knew that the timing would be right, that Asmund might well have gone to ground during those first terrible visitations of the plague.

"Let's check on Google," said Rachel, turning the laptop towards her.

As she tapped away at the keyboard, Will thought he sensed Chris coming back into the room and turned, eager to get the notebook back. But it wasn't Chris, and now Will heard the gentle creaking of the floorboards above, barely audible, as of someone trying not to be heard. He could hear Chris in his study now, so knew it wasn't him.

Rachel and Eloise didn't seem to have heard anything and were busy discussing the villages they were finding on the computer, so Will said, "Is there anyone else in the house? Anyone upstairs?"

Rachel looked up. "No, why do you ask?"

"Nothing, I . . . Do you mind if I take a look?"

She shook her head as if she'd have allowed him anything he requested right then.

Eloise shot him a concerned look, but he stood and said, "It's fine—I'll be back soon."

He walked along the passageway, past the study where Chris was copying pages on a machine that whirred and blinked, up the stairs to a long landing. He stopped and listened, hearing that distinctive shuffling footstep coming from a room, which was probably above where he'd just been sitting.

He opened the door and stepped inside. It seemed to be another study, a small lamp lit on the desk, bright enough that it took a moment for his eyes to adjust. The room was empty, and silent now, too, but Will could feel in his spine that this wasn't just his imagination—something was wrong in this house.

He walked over and looked at the desk, and the wind whistled lightly, having found its way in somewhere, skipping through the upstairs rooms, rattling a couple of the doors. Just as he was wondering if he'd been mistaken about the footsteps, that stray gust of wind picked up some of the papers from the desk and scattered them on the floor.

Once more he felt the chill in his spine as if someone was behind him, and turned, certain he'd heard the same soft footsteps walking past the open door. Again, there was no one there.

Before moving on, Will picked up the papers and placed them back on the desk. They were addressed to Chris and were all on printed notepaper from the same company, the Breakstorm Trust. He glanced through the contents, but it was little more than an educational charity, the sort of thing a wealthy man like Chris might be involved with. If some spirit had meant Will to see this, he couldn't understand why.

He walked back out on to the landing and closed the door behind him and stood for a moment. He could hear no footsteps now, and nothing unusual, but he sensed too strongly that there was someone or something up here and he walked further, finally stopping at a door on his left.

Beyond that door, there was no scent, but certainly a presence. Will listened to the whirring sound of Chris's copying machine down below, Rachel and Eloise talking, then pushed open the door and stepped into the room.

This was a bedroom and a small lamp was lit in there, too—Will wondered if Chris and Rachel were afraid of the dark. But once again, now that he was inside, the room was empty and the presence he'd sensed was gone. There was something ill at ease here, and it was drawing him on, toying with him.

He walked around the room anyway, and finally over to one of the windows that looked down on to the narrow street at the front of the café. And now he knew what presence had been calling him onwards through these rooms.

In the empty street below stood one of the robed women from the cathedral. She stood, her face tipped forwards just enough that it was obscured by the hood of her robe.

Will looked down at her, vaguely aware of his own pale reflection in the glass of the window. It seemed she knew he was watching because she raised one arm and pointed along the street. He looked in that direction, but could see nothing, only the floodlit spire of the cathedral. He wondered if that was it, if she was telling him to return there, warning him perhaps of the dangers he faced at the Whole Earth.

She lowered her arm again, then slowly, for the first time, she lifted her head, and Will understood immediately what Eloise had meant. The spirit only had the shadow of a face, as if her features were covered with a veil of mist, all of them indistinct, only darker patches where her eyes had been.

And then another dark hole appeared in the shrouded face and he realized the spirit had opened its mouth, that even though no sound emerged, the spirit was calling to him. He couldn't understand why, but he took a step back, horrified and disturbed by the sight of this woman, even after everything he had seen in his life.

Behind him, he heard Chris calling, "Is everything okay, Will?"

"Fine," said Will, turning, and when he looked back, he saw with some relief that the woman had gone and the street was empty again.

Chris was waiting for him at the bottom of the stairs.

"I thought I heard someone walking about up here, but it was nothing," said Will.

Chris smiled and said, "Well, we know it's haunted. I expect you're more in tune with that kind of thing than we are." Will nodded and stared at him, trying to read what he could from this young man's eyes. Then Chris smiled, looking embarrassed, and held something out. "Your notebook."

"Thank you," said Will, and they walked back into the other room.

Eloise looked up and said, "Nothing that really fits yet—lots of lost villages, but . . ."

"I'll carry on looking," said Rachel.

"Thank you." Will looked at Eloise and said, "But now we have to go."

She nodded as if she understood and started to put on her coat, stopping only as Chris said, "How will you get there, when you find it?"

He sounded urgent, sensing perhaps that he was about to lose Will, having found him again after all these years. It didn't mean his intentions were bad, and Will wanted to believe in Chris and Rachel, for Eloise's sake as much as anything.

Will said, "What do you mean?"

"You said it's not likely to be in the city, and presumably you can't go about in daylight." Chris smiled and said, "All I'm saying is, when you find out where it is, we'll take you there, if you want us to—any time and place."

"That's very generous," said Will, but offered no more for the time being. He was now sure that Chris and Rachel were bound into this in some way, one more small part of the puzzle that was falling into place, but it was still too soon to know if he could trust them or not.

It was true, some of their behavior had been explained—they had accidentally filmed him in 1989, but he knew nothing else about them, and had no way of knowing what they had done in the intervening years. For all he knew, and until they had proved otherwise, they had sold their souls and were in league with the very forces that sought to destroy him.

19

"You must feel better about them now?" Will and Eloise were walking back along the pedestrianized street that ran most of the way from the café to the church, and it was deserted. The whole city seemed quieter now, and if there had been any violence, there was nothing left to show for it.

"A little."

"A *little*?" She sounded outraged. "You know now why they were acting weird—because they filmed you twenty years ago and here you are looking just the same. And you have to admit, they couldn't have been more helpful."

She was right, and Will was finding it harder to suspect them, but there was still a nagging doubt and he said, "Everything you say is true, but nevertheless, you can't expect me to trust them right away."

"You trusted me right away."

"And was I right to do so?"

"Of course you were!"

"So if my judgment was right in your case, should you not acknowledge that I might also be right to treat Chris and Rachel with caution?"

Eloise groaned with frustration and said, "God, sometimes you really do talk like a seven-hundred-and-fifty-year-old."

Will laughed, but stopped almost immediately, catching a stray scent. And at the same time, Eloise stopped walking and said, "Wow, look at the size of that rat." She was pointing into the shadows, where the buildings met the street, at a large rat running with some determination as if towards the river. "There's another."

But there wasn't just one other—along both sides of the street more rats were following, hundreds of them, all running from the direction of the cathedral, no less than if it was a sinking ship.

Eloise looked up at the night sky and said, "I wonder if there's a fire somewhere."

Will shook his head. "There's no fire." But there was something coming, visible in the urgency of the city's rats, fleeing like a defeated army. "Nature often seems to foresee a catastrophe, sometimes days before it happens. Now that I think of it, something has felt wrong since I killed Jex. And I fear the rats are a sign that we don't have time to waste in finding this church."

"Rachel and Chris . . ."

"Will drive us there." Even as he said it, he wished he could think of some other way to reach the place, sensing that their involvement could only end badly. "But I can't wait for them to find it, and besides, I realize only now that I know where we'll find this information, a place their computers cannot go."

Eloise looked at the rats in the shadows, growing in number, tumbling over each other in their desperation to escape the city and reach the river, running in fear without knowing what it was they feared.

A dog barked in a nearby street, equally spooked. And beyond it, probably beyond Eloise's hearing, Will could hear more dogs barking across the city. No doubt the dogs would have fled, too, if they could. There was a storm coming—of what kind, he didn't know, but a storm nevertheless.

Eloise pointed at the rats and said, "Please tell me we're not going with them."

He shook his head again and started walking onwards as he said, "Have you ever seen the cathedral library?"

"It isn't open to the public," said Eloise.

"It's a thing of beauty, something you ought to see. During the dissolution, the Earl of the time, an unwitting impostor who shared his name with the King, ordered its construction."

A rat collided with another and ran into their path briefly before darting back to the cover of the wall. Eloise's step faltered, but Will didn't break his stride and continued as she ran a step to catch up.

"Henry of Mercia was an interesting character, happy to take the monastic lands, yet equally determined to save the monastic library, containing countless illuminated manuscripts, which would have been lost otherwise. Some of them, of course, have since found their way into my own private collection."

"That's great, but if we're running out of time, we can hardly search a whole library. Google might be quicker."

Will smiled at her impatience and said, "He also commissioned some of the monks to produce two more great works, a pictorial map of his lands and a written account of all the parishes in his realm, a personal Doomsday Book. It's those two works that I think might give us some clues to the church we're looking for."

"Okay, on this occasion Google might not be quicker, assuming you know where to find them."

Will looked at her, bemused, realizing she still had little concept of the years he'd lived, of the emptiness, the night after night of lonely isolation, the sleepless days confined to his chambers. Set against such desolation, the library had become as familiar to him as a favorite toy.

They entered the cathedral through the small side door

and made their way to the caretaker's office. Will picked up the spare key he was looking for, then led the way across the church.

On the far side, he opened a heavy wooden door with the key and led Eloise up a long spiraling staircase and through a small door set in an ornate stone arch. Once inside, he turned on the lights for her benefit and as his eyes struggled to adjust, he waited for her to comment.

She looked around and said, "Er, yeah, it's . . . it's nice." She was disappointed.

Will looked at the long, low room stretching ahead of them, its two walls lined with books, the ancient oak beams arching across its vaulted ceiling. Seeing it from her point of view he could imagine this didn't look like much, but it was only the start of what he had to show her, and although they had a serious purpose here, he found he was desperate for her to love this secret world.

"So first we need to go to the map room." He caught her looking around the apparently simple room, perhaps trying to see where the entrance to the map room might be. "But there's one more thing to tell you before we go. Henry of Mercia was greatly fond of puzzles and riddles."

"Yes! Of course," said Eloise, as if suddenly realizing who Will was talking about. "There's a maze at Marland—it's called Henry's Maze."

"How astonishing," said Will, because as much as he'd tried to keep up with the family history since it had left the city, he'd never heard of the maze. "Astonishing, not least because this library, simple as it looks from here, is a maze in three dimensions. So please try not to become separated, but if you do, stay in the same place and I'll find you."

Eloise nodded, a hint of excitement in her face. He found it reassuring somehow, given what she'd seen in the last couple of days, that she could be excited by the prospect of exploring a library, even one as extraordinary as this.

He led her halfway along the room to a point where the bookshelves gave way on either side to a door.

"Left or right, the choice is yours."

"Left."

"Good." Will led the way through the door, out on to a small wooden bridge, which spanned the darkness. There were lights here and there, but not quite enough to illuminate the complex and twisting shadows that spilled away below them.

Eloise stopped and looked down, staring at another bridge she could see some distance below, running diagonally to the one they were on, and at small balconies and portions of open staircases that emerged in apparently random fashion. And even those balconies possessed their own bookshelves, as if not a single hidden spot was to be left without its treasury of knowledge.

As if conscious of being in a library, Eloise whispered, "This. Is. Amazing. It's like, you know those pictures by Escher?" Will shook his head. "He was this artist who drew all sorts of towers and things with stairs going in a big loop, but every staircase is going up, you know, optical illusions. This looks like an optical illusion."

"I think that was the intention. As you can see, the room we entered first is perched on top of . . ."

"No, don't tell me. I don't ever want to know how this was built. I don't ever want to know my way around—it would ruin it."

Will nodded, understanding her desire to hold on to the mystery of it. He'd seen it constructed, night by night over many years, and yet even he had been full of wonder upon first entering the finished library.

On one of those early visits he'd become disorientated enough to lose his way and had been forced to spend the daylight hours hidden in its literary labyrinth, protected from the sun by the complete absence of windows. And in the course of that day he had encountered only one other person, the old man himself, Henry, his brother's distant descendant, nearing the end of his rule.

But now the library was so familiar, it was as if a three-dimensional map of it existed in his mind, and even if he had not read all the thousands of books hidden within, he was at least familiar with them. He knew where to find them and what to look for.

"Follow me," he said, but almost immediately stopped again. His nostrils flared, picking up a scent, and at the same time he took in what he should have noticed before, that the lights had already been on when they entered.

"What's wrong?"

"There's someone else in here."

"You mean, like a demon or . . ."

He shook his head. "Human."

Right now, a demon might have been easier to deal with, so familiar was he becoming with them.

"But it's the middle of the night. Why would anyone be in here now?"

Those were Will's thoughts, too. Who, apart from him, would be in the library in the middle of the night when the cathedral was closed? And, more importantly, what might they be doing here? Will couldn't help thinking that this late-night intruder might be searching for the exact same thing as Will and Eloise.

20

They crossed a wooden bridge and descended a staircase, moving quickly through a series of small rooms and across another bridge before Will came to a stop. They could now hear the person inside another small room, leafing through a book and talking to himself. He sounded preoccupied enough that he almost certainly hadn't heard their approach.

The room their nocturnal visitor had chosen intrigued Will the most because it was the room that housed Henry's private Doomsday Book, the record of all the parishes in the Earl's lands. Will had suspected they probably weren't the only ones searching for Asmund's lair.

He was relieved that this seemed to have nothing to do with Chris and Rachel. Even if he still couldn't trust them as fully as Eloise would have liked, they'd only just found out about the church without a steeple. So could it be the sorcerer, Wyndham? He was the only other person Will imagined might be searching.

Will turned and gestured for Eloise to stay behind him, then stepped forwards and through the doorway. A man was sitting at the table in the center of the small hexagonal room, and even though his back was almost turned to them, Will could see immediately that it was the huge Doomsday Book he was reading. Was this him? Was this Wyndham?

As if sensing they were there, the man turned suddenly and jumped in fear to the other side of the table. Will was shocked, not by anything in his general appearance—he was a tall, fair-haired man, unremarkable—but because he was a vicar.

The vicar pointed accusingly and said, "You scared the life out of me—what are you doing here?"

Another person might have been thrown, thinking it quite normal for a vicar to be in the cathedral library, even at such a strange time of night. But he was going to great trouble to avoid looking into Will's eyes—it suggested he knew exactly who Will was, and that he'd been told how to avoid becoming mesmerized.

Will was about to respond, but Eloise stepped forwards now and said with incredulity, "Reverend Fairburn?"

Will looked at her. "You know him?"

"He's our school chaplain."

Fairburn pointed a finger at Eloise and said, "So you must know how much trouble you're in, young lady. You're not allowed in here."

"I'll be the judge of that," said Will. He looked directly at Fairburn, even though the vicar still refused to meet his eyes, and spoke slowly to him, determined to draw him out and confirm Will's suspicions. "You know full well that this library and this church belong to me as much as they belong to anybody. And I know full well what it is you search for in that book—the lair of the one who infected me."

"No, no, I . . ."

"More important to me is the matter of who sent you. Who do you serve?"

"You're mistaken. I don't serve anyone and I don't know . . ."

"Did Wyndham tell you what I could do to you if you lied to me?"

"He didn't tell me anything. He . . ." Fairburn stopped, realizing he'd fallen into Will's simple trap. Without saying more, he ran out through one of the other two doors and up another flight of steps.

Will ran after him. Eloise followed after Will, three sets of footsteps echoing across the complex spaces of the library. Then silence descended ahead of them and Will and Eloise stopped. Only Fairburn's scent told Will he was still here.

Will walked forwards, slowly, softly, and Fairburn panicked and started running again. Will stepped out on to a small bridge and saw the chaplain running up an exposed staircase to the right. Will could have leapt from there, but he didn't want to leave Eloise. Anyway, he knew this library too well, and darted across the bridge and up another flight of stairs.

Fairburn, on the other hand, clearly didn't know the library's complexity as well as he thought because a minute later he had reached a dead end, a small balcony he'd mistaken for a bridge. Even as he realized his error, Will and Eloise burst into the small room behind him.

Fairburn heard them and turned, his back pressed against the wooden railings. Will slowed his pace, too, and approached cautiously.

"I mean you no harm—I merely wish for you to tell me about Wyndham."

The chaplain shook his head and said, "I don't believe you. And it wouldn't matter if I did. No, no, it wouldn't—there's only one thing left for me to do." For the first time, he looked up, made eye contact with Will, and smiled with something like relief. Then, as gracefully as someone attempting a difficult high-dive, he tipped himself backwards over the railing.

Eloise let out a small scream as Fairburn's body dropped silently into the shadows. She ran forwards to the balcony, but got there just as Fairburn hit the stone floor far below with a soft thump. Will joined her and looked down at the dark, lifeless outline of the vicar's body.

She stared for a moment, not quite able to take in what she was looking at, then said, "We should check to see if he's still alive."

"He isn't," said Will.

She'd known it herself, and now she said, "Why would someone do that? Why would he kill himself rather than tell you anything about Wyndham?" Before Will could say anything, she answered herself. "Because he's a sorcerer, I suppose. I mean, if he can summon up the dead, who knows what else he's capable of."

Eloise was right, but Will said, "On the other hand, clearly he is no wiser as to Asmund's location than we are, for now at least—all the more reason for us to move quickly. We need to look at the map first, then the Doomsday Book we found Fairburn reading."

At the mention of his name, Eloise couldn't help looking back down into the shadows, and looked sad as she said, "He was a bit of a bore, but harmless enough—it's just hard to believe he was talking to us a minute ago and now he's dead." She shrugged and added, "I suppose you don't really understand that, with all the death you've seen."

"I understand it, but I don't feel sorry for people like Fairburn." He caught the flicker of an objection in her eyes and said, "Eloise, seven hundred years ago I was heartbroken when I realized my father was dead, my brother, my stepmother, so many more besides. That's why I don't feel sorrow for people like Fairburn because my sorrow was all used up. Almost everyone I've ever cared about died a very long time ago."

"Almost?"

She'd understood his use of the word even though he hadn't been conscious of it himself.

"Almost," he said.

She smiled sadly at Will and took his hand in hers and kissed it, her lips soft and warm against his fingers.

"Sorry," she said, as if fearing even that sign of affection might be too much for him.

Will smiled back. He took her hand in response and pressed it against his own lips, and didn't let her see the pain that such a simple intimacy caused to tear through his head.

"I wish . . ."

Eloise hesitated, but he understood what she wished for and he said, "So do I."

She nodded and then put the thought away, saying brightly, "Okay, let's go and look at maps."

He led the way, across bridges and through book-filled chambers and down spiral staircases, before taking one final bridge into the map room. There were no books here, and Eloise looked around at the shelves housing hundreds of rolled maps.

"Don't worry, ours is on the wall."

Will pointed across the room to the vellum map,

protected behind glass and taking up most of one free wall. She walked across and stood close, taking in the detailed drawings of villages and hills, woods and rivers and roads, of the city itself, resplendent in the middle and topped by the cathedral spire.

"Here's Warrham Minor," she said, pointing to a village on the right-hand edge of the map. "That's one of the lost villages Rachel found."

Will looked at the simple but carefully rendered illustration of a church amid a huddle of houses and felt saddened by the knowledge that it had long since disappeared from the map and from the land upon which it had sat for centuries, the endeavors of its people all come to nothing. "So it was still thriving in the sixteenth century, perhaps too late for our village."

"Yeah, and anyway, Rachel said it's a tourist attraction."

He nodded his understanding and went back to looking at the map.

"What exactly are we looking for?"

"We're looking for gaps where once there might have been villages, or churches sitting alone."

Eloise took in his words in silence and pored over the map little by little. After a few minutes she said, "What about here? Look, three roads meet—surely that's the kind of place you would have had a village." He looked at it, realizing the hopelessness of their task, and then Eloise answered her own question, saying, "But that wouldn't work, just being a lost village. We need a church."

"You're right," he said, and as he glanced across the expanse of the map, he couldn't see an isolated church anywhere—all still had villages attached. He hated to think that the church they were looking for might lie beyond the boundaries of this map, for if it did, the danger to him of getting there would be so much greater.

Then his eyes fell on Marland Abbey, the building illustrated on its own, without the additional buildings and cloisters that had surrounded it. One of the monks, perhaps as a bitter joke, had drawn a small guardian angel hovering above the abbey.

Eloise saw him staring and said, "It's a shame, isn't it, that so many things have been lost?"

"It is," he said, unable to take his eyes off the abbey, equally unable to imagine what this whole world looked like now, a world he hadn't seen by daylight for the better part of a millennium.

Eloise went back to her close inspection of the map. Almost immediately, and with a touch of panic, as if she thought it might disappear or she might lose it, she said urgently, "Will, I think I've found something!"

He tore himself away and looked to where she was pointing.

"It's a wood," he said, puzzled. "A large wood, I'll give you that, but a wood all the same."

She wagged her finger at him, beaming as she said,

"Look closely. Part of that wood has been added afterwards! It's covering something up, and if you ask me, it looks like a picture of a church."

Will saw instantly now, as if it should have been obvious at first glance, no less than one of the optical illusions Eloise had talked about. There appeared to be a church on a hill, but in a subsequent attempt to hide it, trees had been drawn over the top of it, incorporating it into an existing woodland.

It was even possible to see that a different hand had painted the more recent trees, which were fussier, more detailed, all the better to conceal what lay beneath. She was right. Someone had tried to hide this church.

"There can only be so many reasons why someone would want to make a church disappear from the records."

"Right now I can think of only one." She got even closer to the glass and Will was just about to ask if she wanted him to open the case when she said, "The name's written underneath it. I can't quite make it all out, but it begins with *P*. Then maybe a *U*?"

"Puckhurst!"

"Yeah, it could say Puckhurst."

Eloise stood up straight, but Will was already scanning the names across the rest of the map, making sure that he hadn't missed the name of Puckhurst anywhere else.

"Do you know it?"

"I never went there, but it was a wealthy village in our time. A fair proportion of my father's revenues came

201

from there. Yet clearly by Henry's time, the church alone survived—we need to see if it's mentioned in Henry's Doomsday Book."

"Show the way." He walked towards the door, but was struck by something else, something even more glaring. "What's wrong?"

"What is a puck?"

"It's used in ice hockey."

"I'm sorry?"

"Er, no, it probably isn't that kind of puck." Eloise thought for a moment and said, "Oh, like Puck in *A Midsummer Night's Dream*—he's a kind of elf or wood nymph, I suppose."

"That's why Shakespeare called him Puck. A puck is, as you say, a mischievous elf or goblin or . . ."

"A sprite," said Eloise, the pieces falling into place. "Asmund waits with the sprites. Puckhurst!"

Will nodded, but said, "I still want to check the book. I want to know what happened there."

"And about the steeple."

"Yes, the more we know, the better prepared we'll be."

They found their way back to the small chamber that housed Henry's Doomsday Book together with several hundred other illuminated manuscripts. Will looked first to see what page Fairburn had been looking at and saw that it was Warrham Minor—so Wyndham was on the right track, even if he hadn't yet homed in on Puckhurst.

The book itself was a beautiful creation, the vibrant

colors and illustrations looking like something from another age even in Henry's time—clearly his aim had been to produce something that looked ancient and spoke of his family's rich history.

But as beautiful as it was, Will turned the pages greedily until he found the small section on Puckhurst. Thankfully, the person who'd tried to remove the place from the map had never found his way to this volume.

Will started to read and Eloise said, "So you *do* know Latin. You told Rachel and Chris you didn't."

"That was before they knew my true identity."

"True. What does it say?"

"It recounts the tragedy of Puckhurst. A steeple was being added to the church, but half-completed, it was struck by lightning and destroyed. A month later, the Black Death descended upon the village and the steeple was abandoned. The population was much reduced. But here's the interesting part—in 1353, when the rest of the land was free of pestilence, Puckhurst alone was struck by a further plague, which lasted for several years until the remaining population fled to the city, abandoning their village to God."

"He's there." Will nodded, and Eloise thought about it for a second before asking, "Are you scared, Will? I mean, do you get scared?"

"I don't think so. I'm uneasy, but then I've been uneasy for seven hundred and fifty years. And I fear myself. I fear that I'll fail to do justice to my name and title."

"Yeah, that keeps me awake at nights, too." Eloise waited for him to smile, then laughed and said, "I'm not scared at all. I believe, one hundred percent, this will turn out right."

Will nodded again, trying to assure her that he felt the same way, but he was thinking of the poor people of Puckhurst, unknowingly bled into extinction by a feudal lord of darkness, Asmund. And he hoped, too, that Eloise couldn't see that he *was* scared, not for himself, but for her.

21

In the late summer of 1256, a curse seemed to fall upon this city and the lands that surrounded it. Rumors came first from a village to the north, of a child and a man who had both been struck down by a strange sleeping sickness.

Throughout the late summer months, more reports came of healthy people meeting their deaths in similar fashion. Some had been bitten, or so the rumors went, and the blood had been drained from their bodies.

Other strange occurrences filled those months. Sheep and cattle were found mutilated, often missing their heads, churches were desecrated, and the dead removed from their graves.

Witchcraft was suspected, and as the weeks progressed and accusations flew from village to village to city, seven unfortunate women were brought to trial. Even though they came from various locations, they were accused of being a coven, found guilty, and sentenced to death by fire.

I have long believed that my father knew as well as I do now that these poor women were innocent, but he was no fool and I cannot condemn him for what he did. There was panic across his entire domain and the people, whether they knew it or not, required a blood sacrifice.

The death of the witches satisfied the population, and as events transpired, the evil acts that had dominated the harvest months came to an abrupt end with the burning. Their Lord had delivered them.

The burning of the witches took place late in the afternoon of the second of October. The weather being fine, and excitement being widespread, people came into the city from outlying villages for the spectacle.

The pyre was built on the small rise close to the West Gate, ensuring that the easterly wind would keep the flames from wreaking the witches' revenge on the buildings of the city.

The seven were tied to posts at the center of the

pyre and left there for an hour as the crowd gathered. I can only imagine the abuse and taunts they suffered in that time.

Certainly, they looked ready to meet their end by the time we arrived with the light fading. As the flames were put to the bonfire, one of the women cried out some confused sermon to the baying crowd, but the others remained silent even as the fire reached them.

The protesting woman yelled one last curse, that her descendants would take this Earldom unto themselves. Then she, too, fell into silence, and I wonder now if the smoke killed them before the fire had started to eat at their flesh. I hope so, for there could be no worse way to die.

I can't remember what I thought of them at the time. I was curious that there was no smell from the fire, perhaps because the wind was against it, but other than that I think I failed to fully comprehend that this magnificent spectacle was bringing about the death of seven innocent women.

The fire burned vigorously, sending glowing embers flying up into the night sky and out into the western darkness. It crackled and filled the land with its orange glow and illuminated the crowd in its ghostly light.

I walked amongst that crowd, I remember that much, but I recall nothing else. At some point I was bitten, at some point my body was found, and I have little doubt that the witches were most probably blamed for one last act of evil.

But the acts attributed to those women must surely have been perpetrated by the man who bit me, Asmund. And though I chose to be bitten no more than they chose to be burned, I can't help but believe that I was somehow responsible for their deaths. I pray only that there was some reason for it, for all of it, that this was done to me for a purpose and that those women did not die for nothing.

Perhaps Asmund himself had no choice in the matter. I can only assume now that he was in the service of Lorcan Labraid, playing his part in what the fates have planned for me. My need for vengeance against him might even seem hypocritical, given the many lives I have ended over these long centuries.

And yet, beyond answers, vengeance is what I desire most from Asmund. I desire it for myself, for the women who were so cruelly condemned for his evil, for the honor of my family and its name. Above all, I desire it because I am the last of the Mercian Earls, the only one left who can put right all the wrongs of that cursed autumn long ago.

22

Will and Eloise both looked up at the ceiling of Chris and Rachel's sitting room as a rogue gust of wind tested the building around them, reverberating through the timbers. They were sitting across from each other on the green sofas and as they lowered their eyes again, Eloise said, "I hope that woman's cat comes back—when this is over."

It was just after eleven on Saturday night and Chris and Rachel were seeing off the last of their customers, not that there were many of them. On their walk through the city, Will and Eloise had found it oddly deserted for a weekend evening and one of the few people they'd met had been a woman looking for her cat.

"I'm sure it will, though I suppose that depends on what *this* is."

"Nature foresees a catastrophe," she said, echoing Will's words of the night before. Another rogue gust of wind pummeled the house and she glanced up briefly. "You're right though. If only we knew what kind of catastrophe it'll be."

She'd misunderstood him and now he said, "Don't you see? The catastrophe is me. My very existence is an affront to everything that is natural and good."

Eloise's response was simple and unshakeable. "I don't believe that."

But before either of them could say any more, they were interrupted by the sound of Chris and Rachel approaching, chatting in a light-hearted fashion. Will's arm started to ache and burn, the stubborn return of that ill omen whenever they were near. They looked innocent enough though—he had to admit that to himself—and happy, too, as Rachel sat next to Will and Chris settled down at Eloise's side.

Immediately, Chris looked across at Will and said, "We've had some success. I'm not making any promises, but I think we've narrowed it down to three possibilities, all within about thirty miles of here."

"Is one of them Puckhurst?"

"Yes," said Chris, puzzled.

"Good, because that's the one. We came here to tell you."

Rachel turned to face him and said, "But how did you find out, and I mean, how do you know that's the one?"

"It's a long story, but I'm absolutely certain that Asmund is in Puckhurst."

"Right now?"

Will nodded and said, "I was hoping you might be prepared to take me there."

"Is tonight soon enough for you?" It reassured Will to hear Chris say that—he didn't try to buy time, whether to lay plans or inform others. Maybe Eloise had been right about them all along.

But Will didn't have time to answer the question. There was a sudden blast of wind, as if one of those rogue gusts had finally prized open an upstairs window. It died away just as suddenly and a book flew violently from the shelves on the far wall and landed with a thump on the coffee table in front of them. It fell open as it landed.

Both Chris and Rachel jumped backwards in their seats, a look of terror on their faces that didn't bode well for them being much help if there were trials ahead. Eloise jumped, too, but immediately rallied herself and said, "What book is it?"

She leaned forwards, but as she reached out, the pages of the volume burst into flames, a fire so intense that it was hard to believe the book hadn't been soaked in some sort of fuel.

Will shielded his eyes from the glare, but he couldn't help but smile, too—this had to be the work of the female spirits, trying to warn him off, but it was only making him all the more determined to unearth Puckhurst's secret.

Rachel jumped from her seat and ran out of the room, coming back a moment later with a jug of water, which she threw over the burning book. The flames died immediately and Chris gingerly brushed away the pages that had been reduced to a black film of ash.

"Well, I never," he said as he revealed the first two surviving pages, each of them bearing a large illustration and only singed around the edges.

"It's my tarot book," said Rachel, glancing at the shelf from which it had flown, then pointing at the two pictures, which had now been revealed, each of a tarot card. "That's the Hanged Man, suspended upside down by one foot. And, of course, Death needs no explanation, though the card rarely refers to death itself."

Will wasn't interested in death. What intrigued him was the picture of the hanged man, and perhaps the position of the two pictures was significant.

"A hanged man, but possibly a suspended king, and to find him means also finding death." He looked at the three of them. "It's a warning—the spirits that did this don't want us to go to Puckhurst."

It was Rachel who responded first, saying, "But do you want to go?"

"Of course."

She looked determined as she said, "Then our car's in the garage out the back—we're ready when you are."

"Do you know how to get there?"

Chris nodded, and they all ignored the flickering of the lights as he said, "Is there anything you need?"

A low rumble of thunder growled ominously across the sky overhead and Rachel laughed nervously. "I was just going to say, how odd, thunder in November, but I don't suppose it's any odder than books spontaneously combusting."

Eloise laughed, too, and said, "I was just thinking exactly the same thing!"

Will was becoming more and more uncomfortable. Their mood was too light, as if they saw this as some great adventure. His real concern was that he was leading them into a greater danger than they realized, and Eloise most of all.

"Do you have any weaponry?" The smiles faded as they stared in Will's direction. He couldn't believe that they hadn't given any thought to the dangers that might lie ahead, but he said carefully, "There are clearly forces that will try to stop me reaching Puckhurst. I can't even be certain that the man I hope to find there will talk willingly, and Asmund is not some ephemeral spirit—he will be as solid as I am and perhaps less well disposed towards the world. So I have nothing to lose, but you should consider carefully before setting out on this journey."

Chris smiled and said, "We can't speak for Ella, I mean, Eloise, but as for Rachel and me, this is the most amazing thing that's ever happened to us." He waved his arms around, gesturing at the books and ornaments that filled the house. "You've seen all this stuff—we've been looking for proof of ghosts or the supernatural for years, and we're not gonna pass up an opportunity like this. No way."

Backing him up, Rachel said helpfully, "We have a samurai sword. We were given it by a Japanese company we did business with in the dot-com days. It's hanging on the wall in the office, but it's a real sword."

"Good, may I borrow it?"

Chris got up as the lights flickered again, and Eloise called after him, saying, "And Chris, do you have any torches?"

"Yeah, but we've also got an electric camping lantern—that might be better."

Will turned to her and said, "I won't need a lantern, and I think I should go into the church on my own."

Eloise looked him straight in the eye with steely determination as she said, "I hate to remind you of this, Will, but did I not help you at least a little with your brother? Did I not find Puckhurst on the map?"

"Detection work and dealing with spirits is one thing, but I fear there's something more evil about the creature we hope to find at Puckhurst than in anything we've yet encountered."

"Then perhaps you need me more than ever. Anyway, I think I've earned the right to come after everything that's happened."

Will didn't respond, realizing how determined Eloise was, how little chance he had of dissuading her. Perhaps he should have mentioned his real fear, that he'd be asked to sacrifice her just as the spirits had suggested, but he didn't remind her of it because he knew it wouldn't sway her, and because a part of him wanted her to be there.

Chris walked in carrying the sword in one hand and the lantern in the other. He handed the lantern to Eloise. Will took the sword and pulled it a little out of its sheath to inspect the blade—light but razor-sharp. "Let's hope we have no use for it."

The lights flickered again as they got up to leave, and as they emerged into the small yard at the back of the house, the wind was gusting violently and the clouds were stacking up with menace in the dark sky above.

Something fell and shattered not far away, a roof tile perhaps. The buildings all around them creaked and groaned. And beyond the edge of the city, the sky flickered with lightning, illuminating the mountains of black cloud looming overhead.

They climbed into Chris and Rachel's Range Rover and set off towards the West Gate. Will and Eloise were in the back and she looked at him now and said, "Have you been in a car before?"

"In the 1980s, a number of times. I wanted to know what it was like so I used to take taxi journeys—it relaxed me."

"I doubt it did the same for the driver," said Chris.

Will smiled and Rachel said, "It's astonishing to think of you traveling around the city in a taxi back when we were students. It seems such a long time ago. Though I don't suppose you see it like that."

"Sometimes everything seems a long time ago."

No one responded at first, and then Rachel started to say something, but ground to a halt as the lights of the city went out, the streets reduced to total blackness. And, a second later, thunder boomed and cracked across the sky above them.

"Must've been a lightning strike," said Chris, though no one believed it was that innocent.

They drove through the West Gate and out through the suburbs of the city, all shrouded in the same inky darkness. And the further they got from the city, the more fiercely the wind buffeted the car and squally rain lashed itself in sheets against the windshield.

Anyone driving for pleasure would have given up and returned home, and Will guessed that was exactly the purpose of this weather, to make them turn back. But Chris slowed down and leaned forwards to peer at the road ahead where their own headlights were the only illumination.

They turned on to more minor roads, single-track and hemmed by hedgerows. The wind ripped at the winter branches and scattered them in front of the car where they snarled under the wheels and clattered away.

The thunder seemed to grow more distant for a short

while, but then lightning blasted down in front of them, exploding into the bare branches of a tree, which fell burning in their path. Still Chris didn't stop, and even accelerated briefly to clear the flames.

But then they rounded a bend and as the headlights illuminated the rain-lashed lane ahead of them, Chris hit the brakes and stared open-mouthed. Will moved into the middle of the backseat to get a better look.

Someone was walking in the road, walking slowly away from them, a woman in a dark hooded robe.

"I don't like this," said Chris.

"Nor me," said Rachel.

They looked back at Will and then he heard Eloise, sounding nervous, but trying to overcome it. "What should we do, Will? Do you think it's one of the spirits we saw?"

He looked at the figure who'd stopped moving as they'd halted. No one would be out walking on a night such as this; no one would ignore a car behind them—only a spirit that was determined to slow their progress. Even so, Will could understand Eloise's hint of doubt because the woman looked very real, even more so than the one who'd appeared in his chambers.

"Drive through her. It's a spirit."

Rachel glanced forwards and said uncertainly, "Are you sure? She looks awfully solid to me."

Will looked at Chris and said, "Trust me, drive through her."

Chris nodded and the car started to move again, building speed. The rain still prevented them from seeing the woman properly, but the closer they got, the more solid she looked, no spirit but flesh and blood.

Rachel shouted, "Chris, stop!"

"Drive through her," said Will firmly.

"Chris, no—you'll kill her!"

Chris ignored Rachel, looking grimly determined, and now they were only seconds away from hitting the woman.

"Will?" It was Eloise, wanting reassurance.

Rachel covered her eyes and shouted again, "Chris!"

And, at the last second, the woman started to turn to face them. Chris slammed on the brakes, but it was too late. The car ploughed into her. But there was no deafening thud. They passed right through her, or she passed through them, the energy shaking the car, and bringing with it a terrifying female scream that clawed at them and tore their eardrums.

Chris stopped braking even before they'd come to a stop, then accelerated again, his knuckles white where they gripped the wheel. Will and Eloise both looked behind them, but there was nothing there to see, even as the echo of the scream still died away.

Will expected this would be the moment they chose to go no further, but Chris screamed himself, an exhilarated sound, and Rachel joined in and then she turned, her eyes wide open as she said, "Can you believe that! I thought

I'd never do anything wilder than bungee jumping but that . . .!"

Will looked at Eloise. She looked calmer, but smiled at him and, guessing he needed an explanation, she said, "It's this sport where you tie a long piece of elastic around your ankles and jump off a very high bridge."

"Oh." He was too confused by their reaction to ask why anyone would want to do such a thing. They had been terrified, he was certain of that, but they had apparently brushed it off as if this, too, was merely a sport to them.

They drove for another ten minutes before a flash of lightning lit up the sky and briefly illuminated a church on a small hill before sending it hurtling back into the darkness.

"That's it," said Rachel. "The turning must be just ahead on the left."

Chris slowed even further and veered onto a narrow track that led down into some woods where the bare branches of the trees danced wildly in the storm. He stopped the car and turned off the engine.

If there was any fear left in them from the encounter with the spirit, they were masking it well. Chris was almost breezy as he said, "It's by foot from here, I'm afraid. But it shouldn't be far."

Will turned to Eloise and said, "I'll say this one last time—I think I should do this alone. You should stay in the car."

It was Rachel who answered. "Will, I don't think it's a good idea for Eloise to stay in the car on her own. You see, we're coming in with you, too."

Will laughed. "I appreciate your support, even your recklessness, but this is my destiny, not yours."

"You don't know that," said Chris. "We all want to go into that church and, you know, I'm not entirely sure how can you stop us, but how do you know that it isn't our destiny, too? You suggested as much yourself. How do you know we weren't meant to film you and that you weren't meant to meet Eloise precisely so that we could walk into that church together?"

Will didn't answer and Rachel said, "There's an extra torch in the back. We'll take that, and Eloise, you take the lantern."

"Okay," said Will, admitting to himself that he could hardly stop them—at least, not in any way that he considered acceptable. "But please, try not to shine the torch or lantern near my eyes. And may God preserve all of you."

"You mean, all of *us*," said Eloise.

Will smiled and shook his head. "If there is a God, He abandoned me a long time ago."

They got out of the car and Rachel pointed the direction uphill through the woods to the spot in the night sky that the church occupied. They started walking, but had only reached the far edge of the trees when the wind and rain grew fiercer, clattering the branches behind them and stinging their faces.

Even Will could feel it pummeling him as he pushed up the hill, but the others struggled to walk at all. Will reached out and took Eloise's hand and helped to pull her forwards.

They battled on like that, fighting the wind and rain for each step. Will was all too conscious that the ground they walked on had once been homes and roads, and that a community had thrived in this barren spot until the plague had claimed it.

Now it was home to only one resident, Asmund himself, but Will could feel the dead here—they were in the soil and the air and in the stones of the building in front of them. He could even hear them and thought at first it was only him, but then he heard Chris shout something.

"Oh my God, what's happening there!"

Will and Eloise turned to look back at Chris and Rachel. They'd ground to a halt and were looking at the grass in front of them, which appeared to be churning. A flash of lightning illuminated the small hill and now they could all see it—the earth was pulsating, the bones of the dead rising to the surface as if clawing their way out, before being sucked back under, their cries and moans coming with them on the wind.

"Just keep walking!" shouted Will. "Don't look at it!"

He didn't wait, but pulled at Eloise's hand again and set off, deafened by the wind and thunder and lashing rain, and by the cries of the dead. And when they finally reached the relative calm of the church porch, he was relieved to see Rachel and Chris just a few paces behind them.

The four of them looked a poor sight, rain-soaked and bedraggled, but Will didn't have time to worry about appearances—Asmund undoubtedly knew they were coming.

Will reached for the heavy black handle on the door and said, "Are we ready?"

They nodded and he stepped into the nave of the church, and only as he walked forwards did he notice that his arm was no longer aching, that the discomfort of the wound had cleared at some point between leaving the car and reaching the church. There was no more need for portents—he had waited more than seven hundred and fifty years for this, and now their meeting was finally at hand.

23

As was to be expected for a church that had been abandoned for more than six hundred years, it was bare
inside, though its status as an ancient monument had
also ensured that it had been well-maintained. It was also
clear that it had once served a prosperous village.

There were broad aisles on either side of the nave,
and because the chancel was distinguished now only by
a small step, the inside of the church seemed cavernous.
At first glance, there appeared no hiding place, but Will
knew there could be many.

Eloise, Rachel, and Chris drifted towards the space
where the altar had once stood at the chancel end, their

lights dancing awkwardly against the pillars and the stained glass of the windows. Will took the other direction and stepped through the archway that led to the tower.

"Wait there, Will." Eloise came back to join him. He thought Chris and Rachel would follow, but they were chasing their torch beam into what he guessed had been the vestry.

"Stay behind me," said Will. He'd already seen the two sets of steps, one leading up into the tower, the other down into the crypt. The thunder cracked and rumbled above.

Will started down into the crypt. He was tempted to draw his sword now, knowing they had already lost any element of surprise, but he resisted, reminding himself that even if Asmund knew they were there, he could hardly know that Will wished him harm. After all, if the prophecies were right, Asmund probably saw himself merely as Will's guide on the next stage of the journey— assuming that Asmund *knew* about his part in the prophecies.

The steps spiraled down and finally opened out into a small empty chamber. Will stepped into the middle of it and though she tried to keep it away from him, the space was so small that he had to shield his eyes from the dancing of Eloise's lantern.

"Sorry," she said.

"It's not your fault." As an afterthought, he said, "Perhaps if you put it on the floor."

She placed the lantern at her feet and he walked around the edges of the small crypt, running his hands along the walls, looking at the floor, searching for signs of an opening into another chamber or a deeper recess. But there was nothing, just this small square space, less than ten paces across. Yet if this crypt was not Asmund's lair— the thought hit home—there had to be another hiding place!

His nerves clawed up on themselves as Will realized he'd made an appalling mistake by allowing them all to come here, by leaving Chris and Rachel up in the church, by not stressing the dangers clearly enough.

As the dreadful truth crystallized in his mind, he said, "There's another crypt!"

He didn't even wait for Eloise, but leapt up the stairs and was only vaguely aware of Eloise running after him, the beam of her lantern chasing him up the spiral steps. Perhaps she was panicked at being left down there alone, but there was no danger behind them, he knew that.

He ran back out into the nave and saw Rachel and Chris, standing on the step of the chancel, facing him. He walked towards them, then stopped abruptly and made ready to draw his sword as he realized they'd been hypnotized.

A part of him was curious—he only ever seemed able to mesmerize people for as long as he remained in their presence. There was no sign of another being in the church, and yet they both looked lost in a deep trance. Their eyes were staring out across the nave as if they were still fixed upon the person who'd mesmerized them.

"Do you look for me, William of Mercia?" The voice was powerful and deep, with the hint of a distant accent.

Asmund was behind him. And so was Eloise. Her lantern clattered to the floor and rolled, sending out whirling spirals of light before coming to rest.

Will turned, realizing too late that Asmund had been hiding in the tower—he couldn't believe he'd been so careless. He saw Eloise first, looking apologetic, as if this was her fault and not his. Then he saw the man who stood directly behind her, his hands resting firmly on her shoulders.

He was perhaps younger than thirty in his person, with sandy blond hair pulled back behind his head, a close beard. He was dressed in the style of a Norse warrior, although his clothes looked as if they'd been acquired from slightly more recent victims.

Most alarmingly, he was large. Eloise was almost as tall as Will, but the top of her head barely reached her captor's chest and he looked twice as wide across the shoulders.

"You don't remember me," said the man, and Will noticed that his canines were long. "My name is Asmund and I was an Earl, too, in another life."

His face wasn't even familiar to Will, and he found it hard to imagine him walking unnoticed among the spectators of the burning all those years before. But walk among them he had because Will knew in his marrow that this was him, and above all, he had one vital question.

"Why did you do this to me?"

Asmund looked puzzled, even offended, and said, "Are you not pleased? I gave you immortality."

"You gave me an eternal half-life."

"A half-life?" He sounded outraged. "Did I not prepare your chambers in every regard? Did I not ensure that you would have an entire city at your disposal? And through the centuries of your *half-life*, I have waited here for this day, surviving on an unfortunate vagrant now and then. Think back over all those years you were active, Will Longshanks, and think on this—I was here, awaiting your arrival, waiting without distractions, with nothing!"

Calmly, Will asked, "Why did you choose me?"

"Choose you?" Asmund was bemused, but in a cruel, hard-edged way. "I didn't choose you. I was sent. You were chosen long before you were even born. I did my master's bidding in biting you and gave you what was rightly yours, just as for more than seven hundred years I have waited to help fulfill your destiny. Not mine—yours. So . . ." He lifted one large hand and stroked Eloise's hair as if patting a dog. "Could you not be even a little grateful?"

"Let her go," said Will with calm authority.

"Oh, she can stay here for a little while." His tone was playful, but concealed a threat. "I like the smell of her."

Changing tactics, and trying to distract him from the thought of Eloise, Will said, "If you'd left me at least some knowledge of my condition, I might not have kept you waiting so long."

Asmund shrugged and said, "That was not my choice to make. Besides, I'm only three hundred years older than you—what makes you believe I have so much more knowledge than you do? I know only what my master instructs me and what I've come to understand for myself."

"And who is your master? Lorcan Labraid? Or Wyndham?"

Asmund laughed menacingly, and for the first time, Eloise looked afraid. Perhaps she'd been afraid from the start—Will found it hard to believe otherwise—but she could no longer conceal it.

"You are a scholar, it seems. The name Wyndham means nothing to me. I serve my master and my master serves Lorcan Labraid, as do we all, but I have never met him."

"But you know who he is?"

Asmund looked down at Eloise and smiled in a way that made Will uneasy, but then he looked up again and said, "Before your people ruled here, before mine, all of this belonged to Lorcan Labraid, a great king, one of the four, and the only one who survives still."

"Is he the Suspended King?"

Asmund shrugged and said, "I've heard it, but that does not matter. All that matters, William of Mercia, is that he calls to you, through me, through others—he calls to you."

"Why?"

"It's not for me to know. All I am permitted to know, all that governs my existence, is that he needs you alive. For centuries I've helped you stay that way, always unseen, and after I tell you the things I must tell you here tonight, my task is finally done."

"So tell me," said Will. "We've both waited all this time—why should we wait any longer?"

Asmund nodded, as if giving the point some thought, but it was clear he had something else in mind. "That is so, it's why we're here, but in the lives of great men there are many tests, and the price for destiny is often high." Will drew his sword in response, throwing the sheath to one side. Asmund looked mildly surprised and said, "You act rashly for someone who has lived so long. I wish merely to remind you that I arose when you did, several days ago."

"What of it?"

"You know my meaning—we're the same, you and I. So have you fed, William?" Will didn't answer. "Exactly, but I haven't and I need blood. It's all I ask, from one of our kind to another: the knowledge I possess in exchange for her blood." He lowered his eyes towards Eloise.

Will was sympathetic, knowing how it felt to need blood and not have it, but even if they were the same kind, and even if he had known Eloise for only a few days and she would most likely die in his lifetime, he couldn't offer up her life for any amount of knowledge. Would he sacrifice her, when the time came? The answer was no.

"Why didn't you feed on them?" He gestured towards Rachel and Chris. "They have plenty left in them. Why her?"

Asmund smiled, malevolent, making clear that it wasn't just about hunger, but about forcing Will to make the one sacrifice he was least prepared to make. "You know yourself, there's blood, and then there's *blood*."

"You and I are not alike. And if this is meant to be a test, then I've failed because I won't let you take her." Even as he said it, another voice in his head was yelling at him to accept the deal, gnawing away with the argument that her life was worth less than his future, but he wouldn't yield. He wouldn't surrender her.

"I can make her one of us," said Asmund. "You don't have that power, but I do."

Astonishingly, Eloise, who'd looked terrified until now, looked urgently hopeful and tried to catch Will's eyes with her plea, a silent repeat of her wish to be made like him. But he knew instinctively that Asmund was lying, that he had no more power than Will to transform people, and after all these centuries, he finally knew why.

"Asmund, you've just helped me understand something that's puzzled me across the ages. I see only now that you and I became like this because it was already within us."

Asmund smiled and said, "It's taken you all this time to understand that, why you're drawn to some healthy people and not others? You thought it was a choice? Did it never occur to you that you *chose* not to feed off some people because, deep down, you knew their blood would give you nothing, that your bite would only awaken within them what mine awoke within you? Yes, it is in our blood from the beginning, and but for me you would have died a normal death without ever knowing it."

Will was as amazed by this realization as he was embarrassed at having remained blind to it for so long. This had been in him from the start, just as it was in many others, most of whom would live and die in happy ignorance of their inherited "gift." But one thing had not changed—Eloise was not one of those people.

"If you bite Eloise, she'll die, and I repeat, I won't allow you that life. I would sooner kill you and live in ignorance."

"Then you will never know the truth. You'll be destined for nothing, condemned to this same existence across thousands of years." As he spoke, his hand slid down Eloise's arm, and Will had the feeling that he would try to tear at the limb before Will could intervene, so determined was he, or so great had his craving become. "When all civilizations have perished and the land has become barren, you will remain, alone, dying inside for the lack of victims on which to feed."

Asmund yanked at Eloise's arm, pulling it towards

his mouth. Eloise screamed, but Will was ready and immediately lunged forwards, swinging the sword for Asmund's neck. It worked in as much as he let Eloise go, so suddenly that she fell to the floor and immediately scrambled away towards the nearest pillar. But to Will's amazement, Asmund caught the blade of the sword in mid-flight.

Will didn't hesitate. He quickly pulled the sword from Asmund's grasp and stepped back a couple of paces. Asmund's hand looked undamaged, even with the sharpness of the blade, but he looked furious.

His voice was full of contempt as he said, "You fool! You would discard your own future to save a girl!" He looked up at the roof then, taking a deep breath before saying, as if to someone unseen, "Enough! I refuse. A thousand years I have done your bidding, but no more, not for this ingrate!"

It was his master he was calling and his master apparently heard because Asmund's face instantly became racked with pain, and he held his head as if trying to prevent it from blowing apart. This was his punishment for his act of defiance, but the torture only seemed to increase his anger and his determination.

Will saw there would be only one outcome, and that one of them at least would perish here tonight. And even if fortune favored him, he knew now that vengeance wouldn't be enough, that killing Asmund would still leave him unsatisfied because he'd come here to learn something far greater than the fragments Asmund had given him.

It infuriated him to know that he'd been so close to finding the truth of what Lorcan Labraid wanted from him, his destiny, the answers he'd been yearning for all these centuries. He was giving up all of it for a girl he'd known only days, and ironically, it was a desire for the same girl's blood that had persuaded Asmund to turn his back on his part in that destiny.

"Hurt me as much as you will," shouted Asmund to the heavens. "But when the boy is dead, you'll have no more hold over me!"

He took his hands away and inhaled deeply, breathing through the pain, then reached over his shoulder and drew an enormous broadsword that he was wearing on his back.

"The girl or you," he said through clenched teeth.

"Me," said Will, and lunged, the samurai sword immediately piercing Asmund's body.

Asmund looked down and nodded approvingly, but jumped nimbly back off the blade and said, "You have a lot to learn, and very little time in which to learn it."

He swung the broadsword with terrifying speed. Will managed to duck beneath the blade, but in one fluid motion, Asmund swung back and hacked diagonally. Will jumped backwards and the blade rang like a bell against the stone floor.

He had only a moment, but he ran around the nearest

pillar and leapt at Asmund from behind, trying to use his agility against the might of the broadsword. He struck at Asmund again, trying for the side of his neck, but the larger man swung effortlessly around and the broadsword smashed explosively against his own.

Will watched as one half of the samurai blade broke off and flew through the air with such force that it became embedded in the stone of one of the pillars. He noticed Eloise, too, running behind the pillars to the vestry end of the church, passing the still frozen Chris and Rachel on the way.

Will hurled the remains of his sword the way he'd once seen a knife thrower hurl a blade at the circus. It struck Asmund in the chest, and even with a broken blade, it buried itself deep.

Asmund nodded again, and as he pulled the broken sword from his chest and threw it to one side, he said, "Now *that* was almost a good idea! If it had reached my heart, it might have caused me problems. So perhaps I could have made a warrior of you yet."

"You think yourself a warrior? I was a boy when I was bitten. What excuse did you have? Could you not fight off your attacker, a man of your stature?"

Asmund laughed and said, "If you knew my master, you'd understand the foolishness you speak. He . . ." He stopped, smiling as he realized the trap Will had tried to lead him into, getting him to reveal the things he'd come here to discover. He looked as if he was about to say something else, but suddenly swung the sword again, a swift and vicious stroke.

Will darted back behind the pillar and ran into the center of the nave, standing just in front of the step on which Rachel and Chris were perched. He saw Eloise and then realized that she was throwing something to him. He caught it—the torch—and turned.

Too late. Asmund was standing ready. He grabbed hold of Will's coat at the chest and lifted him off the ground, holding him at arm's length. Will immediately turned on the torch and fired the beam directly into Asmund's eyes.

He screamed, a deep, booming scream that would have drowned the thunder. And he cursed in his own ancient language, but at no point did he loosen his grip or lower his arm.

Will couldn't reach him and knew it was useless to hit him with the torch. He was trying desperately to think what else he could do when Asmund pulled him closer and sank his fangs with lightning speed into Will's hand. The torch dropped to the floor and Asmund loosened his bite, but before he could extend his arm again, Will seized his opportunity.

He swung his fist hard into the side of Asmund's head, then delivered a second shuddering thump to the other side. It worked, the blows so powerful that Asmund dropped him and staggered back a pace or two.

But even as Will fell to the floor, he knew he'd only

have moments before Asmund recovered. He spotted the remains of the samurai sword and scurried towards it. Once it was in his hand, he spun around, still on his knees—Asmund had gone.

He turned again, but saw nothing, only a blur of vision before he felt the force of Asmund's foot blasting into his face. The kick knocked him to within a few meters of the chancel step. He tried to get up, but found himself briefly unable to move, so great had been the impact, and then he couldn't move at all because Asmund stood over him, one foot resting heavily on the base of Will's chest.

As Will looked up, Asmund appeared even more of a giant, and it seemed ridiculous now that he'd ever hoped to defeat him in combat, a man who'd probably been a fearsome warrior even before developing the strengths they both shared.

Asmund seemed to be catching his breath, but Will knew that he was actually fighting through the pain that came with defying his master. And when he spoke, his words were labored, his jaw muscles making an agony of each movement.

"Sunlight and fire will make you wish for death, but won't kill you. The stake, as I believe you know, will imprison you. But there is only one certain way to kill our kind—chop off our heads."

He drew back his broadsword, ready to strike. After nearly eight centuries, the moment had come and Will prepared himself for death, overtaken with a mixture of fear and overwhelming relief that it would end at last. He regretted only that he could do no more to protect Eloise, and as if to emphasize that regret, she called out now.

"Stop!" Her voice was surprisingly firm, but still sounded small and faint after the clatter of fighting. Yet Asmund lowered the sword again and laughed to himself, amused enough to allow the diversion. "Take my blood. Let him live and you can have my blood."

Will answered her, shouting, "Eloise, run, now! Get to the car and drive away."

"I can't drive."

"Perhaps you could try!"

"I'm staying," came her defiant answer. "And the offer stands."

Asmund shook his head. "Too late, girl. I kill him first, then take your blood, not one or the other. Both. And he was telling you the truth—you die tonight. *We* walk through death, we are gods, but you are nothing more than food."

Will felt his hand tightening around the hilt of the broken samurai sword in anger. He felt ashamed that he had been about to go to his death so willingly and that he had so very nearly left Eloise to this monster. He felt ashamed, too, because he realized he would have been sacrificing her just as much by dying as if he'd given her up willingly.

"I'm ready," he said. "Do your worst."

"As you wish," said Asmund, and raised the sword a second time.

Eloise screamed, but Will was ready now and determined, and in the brief moment that the broadsword threw Asmund's balance, he drove the broken samurai sword into his calf muscle and pushed up as hard as he could, shoving the foot up off his chest.

Asmund crashed to the floor, the broadsword smashing down next to him, but still within his grip. Will sprang to his feet and immediately kicked at Asmund's hand, sending the heavy weapon clanging across the nave, dangerously close to Chris's legs.

Will scrambled after it but as he turned with the broadsword in his hands, it was no surprise to find Asmund already recovered enough to be standing facing him just a few meters away. The samurai blade was still skewering his lower leg and he reached down and pulled it out as if it was little more than an inconvenience.

He laughed again, mocking Will, pretending to throw the broken sword. Then, as if to prove that he had nothing to fear, Asmund studied the thin blade, rubbing his finger along it before throwing it carelessly aside. He reached instead to his belt and pulled free a battleaxe.

"How I separate your head from your body is of no importance." Will could hear Eloise behind him and off to one side, fumbling with something or other, and the noise was distracting him, making it hard to concentrate on studying Asmund's movements. "Come then. Be a warrior!"

He sprang violently towards Will, the axe arm trailing behind him as if ready to swing a blow with the full force of his body. Will raised the sword, realizing that he'd have to strike before Asmund got too close, that his timing would have to be perfect. And then he knew what Eloise had been fumbling with because, once again, a light scorched into Asmund's eyes.

His step faltered, only for a moment, but enough. Even as he charged towards him, Will swung the broadsword with a fierce sweep. For a fraction of a second, he thought he'd missed, but then he felt the satisfying resistance of flesh and bone as the blade sliced through Asmund's neck.

Asmund's head flew into the air at the same time as his body crashed into Will, knocking him to the ground and pinning him down. The head never landed, and no sooner had Will crunched onto the stone floor than the body on top of him disappeared into a dazzlingly cold blue flame, which died immediately away.

Even the sword in Will's hand disappeared. It was as if everything that had been connected with Asmund had been sucked away into another dimension by the very act of beheading him. So this was how their kind met their end, and how one day his real death might come to claim him.

He was torn from his thoughts by astounded voices behind him.

"What happened?"

"Oh my God, that was so . . ." It was Chris and Rachel,

released from their spell. He heard their voices, but didn't comprehend their words, then heard Eloise speaking to them, but couldn't quite focus on what she was saying either.

He sat up and heard something fall from his chest on to the floor in front of him. It seemed not everything of Asmund's had disappeared. A metal pendant, its strap cut by the sword's blade, had survived. Will slipped it into his pocket, then stood to face the others.

They stopped and looked at him. Eloise looked as if she wanted to run to him, but she stayed where she was and said, "Thank you."

"For what?" Will was astonished. "It's me who should thank you, for blinding him, for offering to sacrifice yourself."

She smiled a little and said, "I knew you wouldn't let that happen." She looked almost embarrassed and turned to Chris and Rachel. "How much of that did you see?"

"All of it," said Chris, and then to Will, "Sorry, we were completely useless."

Rachel said, "It was horrible, like we were trapped in ice and could see everything happening, but couldn't . . ."

She stopped in mid-sentence and stared over Will's shoulder, alarmed. Chris and Eloise followed her gaze and adopted the same look of alarm. And even before he turned, Will could feel that the atmosphere had changed, that it was distorting in some way or other.

By the time he turned, six women had already emerged

from the walls of the church, three on each side, their robes like ragged mist, their faces pale and almost entirely featureless, only faint shadows to suggest where once there had been eyes, mouths, noses.

They now stood silent guard between the pillars and a seventh woman emerged from the archway at the tower end of the church. She half floated, half walked along the nave until she stood facing him a few meters away. It was the spirits from the cathedral, the ones who'd been so fearful that he would sacrifice Eloise.

For a moment, the seventh woman appeared frozen, but then the shadowy remains of her mouth opened and she said in a detached, otherworldly voice, "Beware, William of Mercia, you heeded not our warnings and you can no longer turn back, but the path ahead is strewn with danger, to you, and to those who travel with you. This is but the beginning. The legions of the underworld await you, armies will seek to destroy you, but only you can know the true course."

"Why have you tried to help me?" Will wasn't even sure that they had tried to help him, but he was certain at least that they meant him no harm.

"We serve another," said the woman.

"Who?"

She didn't answer, but said instead, "Remember, William of Mercia, sever the head and the body will fall."

She began to turn, but Will asked urgently, "Who is Lorcan Labraid?"

The air seemed to crackle as if it was electrically charged. The other six women looked charged as well, as if they might suddenly explode into flames. The woman turned back to face him and after another eerie pause, she spoke again.

"He is the evil of the world, but you know this already. Beware, William, he calls to you and you cannot help but answer."

"But what does he want, and why has he waited till now, why all this time?"

"Just as planets must align, so are you but half of what he needs."

She turned her head, staring at something over Will's shoulder, briefly transfixed by it. Will turned, too, and saw that she was staring at a slightly alarmed Eloise. By the time he faced forwards again, the woman was walking away from him.

More questions tumbled over in Will's head, but he couldn't put any of them into words. The six women were already disappearing into the walls, and the seventh was almost back at the archway that led to the bell tower.

And then it came to him—the seven women, the strangely melted features. "I'm sorry," he called out. The woman stopped and turned. "I'm sorry for what we did to you."

She turned to face him again, and appeared to consider his apology before bowing her head in acknowledgment, and within a few seconds more, she had disappeared into the night's fabric.

"They were the witches, weren't they?" It was Eloise. He turned and nodded.

Rachel looked from Eloise to Will and said, "The witches who were burned?"

"I think so. And yet it seems they were trying to protect us, even me."

"I'm sure they had good reason," said Chris, trying to sound relaxed, but unable to conceal his true feelings—he was scared, so deeply that it would probably never leave him. He looked around the church and tried to adopt a casual tone again as he said, "Speaking of which, do we have any good reason not to be getting out of here?"

Will shook his head and said, "No, let's go."

They recovered the lantern and torch, and the remains of the samurai sword and stepped out into a transformed night. The world was calm again and stars were faintly visible, dimmed only by the light of the moon, which was close to full.

As they walked down the hill, Will looked at his hand. The wound had already healed and Asmund's fang marks were only just visible, the last physical remnants of his existence.

Asmund had poisoned his life, and those of countless others, and in a final act of madness had tried to kill the person he had been ordered to serve. He had probably been a bad person even before the sickness, and yet even though Will had come here in the very hope of destroying him, he felt sad for him now.

He wasn't sure why, whether it was because Asmund had been cursed just as much as he had, or perhaps he was saddened by the loss. For whatever his faults, Asmund had been the first of his own kind that he'd ever met, and together they might have had much to discuss. And Asmund had made him what he was, whether he liked it or not, so in some strange way, perhaps it was the sadness of a boy who has lost his father.

24

An hour later, they were sitting around the heavy wooden table in Chris and Rachel's rustic kitchen. The room was lit by candles because they had returned to find the city was still blacked out from the earlier storm. There was only one candle on the table itself and Rachel had placed it as far away from Will as possible.

Chris had just opened a bottle of red wine and poured out three glasses, saying, "I'm not sure we should be encouraging you to drink, Eloise, but under the circumstances . . ."

"That's very sweet of you, Chris, but I've been drinking wine with dinner since I was about five."

He handed her the glass and said, "Will, I feel awful not being able to offer you anything."

Will shook his head, dismissing the thought, but then Rachel added, "And it's dreadful that you didn't really find what you were looking for."

"But we did find some answers," said Eloise. "At least we know for sure now that Lorcan Labraid is the Suspended King, and that he's one of the four."

Chris shook his head and said, "But each answer just leads to more questions. Who are the four, and how is Labraid a Suspended King, and most of all, *what* were you meant to find out there tonight?"

Will didn't respond and after a second, Rachel said, "You don't look very disappointed, Will."

"I found the man who did this to me. If I never learn anything else about myself, I'll be satisfied that I found Asmund and saw him destroyed."

Eloise sipped at her wine and said, "The way he just vaporized like that—I know he wasn't a nice person or anything, but I felt sorry for him when that happened."

"So did I," said Will, but then remembered the pendant. He took it out of his pocket and looked at it, saying, "This fell from his neck and landed on my chest. It was the only bit of him that didn't disappear."

Rachel took it from him and said, "Looks like bronze. Hey, maybe it was meant to survive. Maybe it was even meant to land on your chest."

look at all familiar?" Without waiting for an answer, he asked Will, "Do you think this is old? I mean, if Asmund had it . . ."

"I don't think he'd left Puckhurst for centuries, and I can't imagine it was delivered to him in that time."

Rachel saw what Chris had been hinting at now and said, "Ley lines! But if this is old, that means Watkins was right." She turned to Will and said, "In the 1920s, an amateur archaeologist called Alfred Watkins came up with the theory of ley lines, the idea that ancient sites were all constructed along certain alignments, connected to the energy in the earth."

The theory sounded vaguely familiar, and Will wondered if he remembered it from that time.

Chris smiled and said, "But, more importantly, I recognize this—that small triangle in the middle is the give-away. These particular lines are very close to here. They cross in such a way that a small triangle of land exists between them, and on that land is Marland Abbey."

"Oh. My. God." They looked at Eloise who explained herself by saying, "This is just too freaky."

Will agreed. "It's certainly a coming together."

"How so? I mean, I know it became the family seat for the Earls of Mercia, but surely that was hundreds of years after your time?"

"But my father . . . I think he had some special connection to that place, something he also instilled in me—I went there many times as a child."

"And I go to school there."

Rachel looked surprised and said, "You go to Marland Abbey? So how come . . . ?"

She was about to ask how Eloise had ended up living on the streets, but Eloise said, "Don't ask, it's all incredibly stupid and embarrassing. But it looks like I ought to go back now, if they'll take me."

"Yes," said Will. "I admit to being curious anyway, for many reasons, but this pendant suggests that Marland is the place I need to go next, though preparing the way won't be easy."

"Maybe not. But we can help, and Eloise will be in the school—hopefully—so that should allow some freedom of movement."

"If they don't have me in solitary confinement," joked Eloise.

Rachel added to Chris's comments, saying, "And Will, if there's nowhere suitable for you there, we can take you out there at night and bring you back, as often as you want—it's not a long drive from the city."

"Thank you. Of course, I'm hoping that won't be necessary. You've done enough already." And in truth, he felt a little guilty accepting their help because he'd suspected them so strongly, led astray by the discomfort in his arm.

Rachel said, "Will, partly thanks to you, the paranormal has been the great passion of our life. We could never do enough if it meant finding out more about all of this. We'd do anything."

He believed her of course, just as he should have listened to Eloise from the start, because they'd already
risked their lives for him and here they were expressing a
willingness to do whatever it took. Perhaps they were just
wealthy people in need of excitement, but whatever they
were, he now doubted they'd ever had a suspicious motive
in their lives.

And as if to prove his natural enthusiasm, Chris said,
"There's just one thing I don't understand. Well, as a
matter of fact, I don't understand anything, but there's
one thing particularly puzzling me."

"Go on," said Will.

"Asmund bit you. His master, for whom we don't
have a name, bit him. And his master's master is Lorcan
Labraid."

"Who's the evil of the world," added Eloise helpfully.

"But you see, that means we've accounted for everyone
in a direct line from you to this ultimately evil creature,
Lorcan Labraid. So if we've accounted for everyone, who
on earth is Wyndham?"

"I wish I knew," said Will. "Someone powerful enough
to raise the dead, a sorcerer, but not apparently connected to Asmund or Lorcan Labraid. Nor is there any
reference to him in Jex's notebook. The only thing we
know for certain about him is that he's dangerous."

Eloise nodded in agreement, but then studied her watch
by the candlelight and said, "Will, I think we'll have to go
soon."

He glanced up at the clock and said, "Of course."

But Rachel got up first and said, "Wait there a minute."

She went through to the other room and came back a moment later with a thin leather strap. She threaded it through the half of the pendant that had been Asmund's and handed it to Will.

"With all this danger around, I think both of you should wear these. They might bring you luck."

"Maybe you're right," said Eloise, and put hers on. Will followed suit, though he was reminded in the process of what had happened to the pendant's previous owner— it had certainly afforded him no protection.

They said their good-byes and Will and Eloise set out into the darkened streets, lit with only the faintest blue tinge from the moon, which was already low in the sky.

They hadn't walked far when Eloise said, "When I thanked you in the church, you asked me what for. So I'm thanking you again." He looked at her questioningly. "When the time came, you chose my life over your destiny—that can't have been an easy thing to do."

"You know, the odd thing is, I hardly even thought about it. I should have done, but I just knew it was the right thing to do. Perhaps Chris was right—perhaps the prophecy referred to what actually happened up there and not what we'd expected."

Eloise laughed. "Well, let's hope some of the other prophecies are a little more straightforward."

They walked in silence for a while. Will thought about

the pendant, about the way those two halves had fused perfectly together, and that in turn made him think of the last few days, which had been the most extraordinary in even his eventful life.

"Why are you smiling?"

He glanced at her and said, "Because I'm happy."

"I gathered, though I can't think why, given tonight's mixed results." Another couple of paces were covered in silence. "Would you like to share the secret of this happiness?"

He touched the pendant with his hand and said, "This has made me understand something. I've been wondering on and off over these last few days, why now, why Jex's notebook, why the emergence of all these strange forces, my brother, the witches, Asmund? Is it because of the new millennium or because of some alignment in the heavens? Why have I waited seven hundred and fifty years and now, all at once, my destiny is being set out before me like a test?"

"And?"

Will stopped walking and she stopped, too, and looked back at him.

"What the witches said. It's because of you, Eloise. The pendant confirmed what I already sensed in every fiber of my being—I've waited seven hundred and fifty years for you to be born. We were meant to find each other because in some way or other—and I don't know what that is—you are part of my future."

253

She stared at him in disbelief, then let out a single laugh, then another. She looked infectiously happy.

"If I didn't taste like dinner, I'd kiss you right now."

"If you didn't taste like dinner, I'd kiss you back."

"Really?"

"Of course. I'm amazed you even need to ask."

He reached out and brushed her cheek with the back of his fingers and she said, "You could hold my hand, unless it hurts for you to do that . . ."

He shook his head and took her hand in his, and as if a memory of his former life had found its way back, this time the warmth of her skin was as restorative as that summer day he dreamt of.

He smiled and they walked on like that, and suddenly the lights burst back into life all around them as the power surged back through the city. They burned so brightly that Will immediately thought to reach for his sunglasses, but he left them in his pocket.

He knew he wasn't the only one who'd waited seven hundred and fifty years for her, but the floodlit cathedral soared reassuringly into the dark sky ahead of them, and on this night, walking with Eloise, it was hard to believe there could be any evil in the world, or that anything could harm either of them.

25

I was different from birth. In my coloring, I took
after neither parent, for both were fair. Indeed, I was
once told that despite my mother's unquestionable
honor, had it not been for the obvious facial resem-
blance to my father he might well have considered
himself cuckolded.

My stepmother told me that my dark hair and
green eyes were the memories of ancient lines
emerging again. That good woman understood well
the complex strands that combine to make us what
we are, as can be seen in the Earldom itself.

My father was no relation to the Anglo-Saxon

Earls of Mercia. He was of Norman descent and inheritor of a title that had been recreated only in 1175 by the grace of Henry II.

Yet my mother was a direct descendant of Edwin, the last Anglo-Saxon Earl. And my stepmother told me of a further link, of the way in which one of Edwin's ancestors had married into the line of the ancient British kings who had ruled here previously—it was from that stock that she claimed I must have derived my dark locks.

I have existed long enough to know something of genetics, to understand complexities that even she might not have grasped. But I have also existed long enough to understand that I possessed something that had belonged to neither my father nor the mother I never knew.

Just as the ley lines converge on the broken pendant, so the noble lines of all the peoples to rule in these islands converged on me. All those ancient rulers, lost beyond the edges of history, have their life force carried like a torch in my person.

And if those noble lines converged once, they must also have threaded through the centuries, crossing and separating, crossing and separating, touching countless others, perhaps even you who read this. For that is something else I have only come to truly understand in the most recent past.

As strange as I might seem, and whatever fate awaits me, we are all born of the same stuff. I am part you, and you are part me. We are blood, you and I. We are blood.

26

It was early evening on the Heston Estate. Sadly, despite borrowing one of the names of the local aristocracy, this was no country park. The Heston Estate was a sprawling mass of some eight hundred houses on the eastern edge of the city.

The houses were run-down; stray dogs roamed the area, gangs of boys could often be seen loitering on street corners, looking for any kind of trouble that might alleviate the boredom.

On this particular evening though, the streets were empty because they were being lashed by a hard, cold rain coming in from the east. So no one was there to witness the large black Mercedes limousine that crawled slowly around the estate, the wet roads hissing gently beneath its tires.

The driver was having trouble finding the house he was looking for, partly because of the weather, partly because all the houses looked exactly the same in the darkness and few of the street signs were intact. His passenger, hidden behind tinted windows in the back, was not concerned.

Meanwhile, in 26 Mandela Crescent, Jane Jenkins was watching a soap on television and wondering if she should do something about Mark. Mark Jenkins was her son, fifteen years old, in trouble for about ten of those fifteen years and the only other permanent resident of this house.

He was up in his room at the moment, and the problem wasn't the kind she was used to tackling. For the last week or so, he hadn't wanted to go out; he'd been polite, a lot quieter than usual, and lost in thought a lot of the time. But he'd also done whatever she'd asked him to do around the house, which wasn't like him at all.

In short, in the last week, Mark had become the perfect kid, and that was worrying Jane, so much so that she almost wanted the old Mark back, even with all the headaches he caused, all the problems with the school, the police calling, hanging around with Taz and the rest of that gang. What really scared her was the possibility that he was doing some weird new drug.

The doorbell rang, and for good measure, a knock

followed immediately after. With some difficulty, she forced herself up off the sofa and went to the door, taking a quick look in the hall mirror before opening it—she didn't look bad for thirty-three, though she guessed she could do with losing a pound or twenty.

She opened the door and immediately took a step back. Two men in suits stood there—one younger, quite tasty, holding an umbrella for an older guy with short gray hair and pale skin and amazingly blue eyes. She guessed the older guy was about sixty, but he'd probably been a catch twenty years earlier.

"Mrs. Jenkins?" His voice was friendly and moneyed, a luxurious drawl to it, definitely too classy for him to be a policeman or a truant officer—that was a relief.

"Miss, actually. Or Jane."

He smiled warmly and said, "How do you do, Miss Jenkins. My name is Phillip Wyndham and I'm here as a representative of the Breakstorm Trust. May I come in?"

Immediately suspicious, she said, "What's it about? If you're selling stuff, you're wasting your time."

"I can assure you, Miss Jenkins, I'm not selling anything. It's about Marcus."

She nodded and said to herself, "Thought it was too good to be true." She stepped aside to let Mr. Wyndham and his driver into the house before saying, "It's Mark, by the way. Marcus was just me going stupid when he was born, and he hates it."

"As you wish," said Mr. Wyndham, and looked around

the small sitting room, which was well looked after, if a little boldly decorated for his tastes. It was also dominated by a very large television on which the volume was deafening.

As if sensing his discomfort, Jane found the remote and turned off the sound before saying, "Sit down. I'll get him." She walked to the bottom of the stairs and let out an ear-splitting scream, "Mark!"

She walked over and sat down opposite Mr. Wyndham, and without prompting, she said, "I knew there was something wrong. I think that Taz is no good. I've said he's not a good influence, but Mark hasn't even wanted to see him this last week, and that's weird."

Mr. Wyndham smiled, though he had little idea what she was talking about, and said, "I think you misunderstand, Miss Jenkins. Marcus . . . Mark isn't in trouble. I'm here as a representative of the Breakstorm Trust to offer Mark an amazing opportunity. You see, the trust is an educational charity, and through our contacts in schools and the community, we select people of exceptional abilities who haven't had the opportunity to shine, and we . . . well, we give them that opportunity."

As Mr. Wyndham had been speaking, the boy himself had emerged from the hall and stood looking at the older man. He wasn't particularly striking to look at, little different to most of the other boys on the estate. The only distinguishing feature was the ghost of a scar on his left cheek.

Mr. Wyndham turned and saw him standing there. He smiled and said, "Ah, I'm guessing this is the young man in question. Hello, Mark."

"Marcus," said the boy, correcting him.

Mr. Wyndham smiled, as much at Jane Jenkins's expression as at the boy's response.

"Hello, Marcus."

"Hello," said the boy and, stepping forwards, shook hands with both Mr. Wyndham and the driver. This was exactly the kind of weirdness that had been so troubling Jane, first with the "Marcus" and then with the hand-shaking—normal boys of his age didn't shake hands and say hello to men in suits. "What's the amazing opportunity you were talking about?" His voice was surprisingly relaxed and unfazed.

"Well, if you and your mother approve, you'll go on a weeklong course to help acclimatize you, then you'll get to go to a leading private school and finish your education there. All the fees will be paid by the Breakstorm Trust, which will also provide an annual bursary to cover more general expenses."

Neither the boy nor his mother fully understood what Mr. Wyndham had just said, but they both got the gist of it. At least, Marcus had.

Jane said, "Is it a TV series? You know, like *Boot Camp* or whatever they call it."

Mr. Wyndham smiled politely and said, "No, Miss Jenkins, this is very much real life. If you agree—and we'll continue to consult you and support Marcus at every step along the way—his life could be completely transformed."

Jane shrugged and said, "He's done what he wanted since he was born—I'm not gonna interfere now. Whatever Mark wants, I'm cool with that."

Mr. Wyndham turned once more to the boy and said, "How about it, Marcus? How would you like to complete your education at Marland Abbey School?"

"Is it a boarding school?"

"Yes, you'll be boarding." He turned to Jane and explained. "We feel it's best for him to make a complete break, at least to begin with."

Jane nodded. She imagined she'd probably miss having him around the place, but she couldn't see him going off to some expensive school and coming back to Heston every night in a weird uniform.

"Okay, I'll go."

"Excellent," said Mr. Wyndham, looking thoroughly delighted. "You know, Marcus, I think you're exactly the kind of young man the Trust has been looking for. I just know you'll achieve everything we want you to achieve in your time at Marland Abbey."

Marcus didn't respond, but idly traced his finger along the faint white scar on his cheek—sometimes the scar bothered him, and this was one of those times. He knew why, too. He'd known something was coming, he'd sensed it for days, and he guessed this was finally it.

As for Mr. Wyndham, he knew exactly what potential Marcus Jenkins possessed and was convinced that he'd make a trusty foot soldier in the struggles to come. He was also certain of another thing—that the time of those struggles was undoubtedly at hand.

He'd waited patiently for two hundred years, but the prophecies were finally being fulfilled. Evil was at large in the world, and it was his duty to seek it out and destroy it wherever it was to be found. The forces of good had to triumph, and above all, he would not rest until he had destroyed the devil-child himself, that thing of darkness, seat of evil, William of Mercia.

Coming from Egmont USA in Fall 2012

Alchemy

Book Two in the Mercian Trilogy